The House Swap

Also by Yvette Clark
Glitter Gets Everywhere

YVETTE CLARK

HARPER

An Imprint of HarperCollinsPublishers

Library of Congress Control Number: 2022940761
ISBN 978-0-06-303453-2

Typography by Chris Kwon
23 24 25 26 27 LBC 5 4 3 2 1

First Edition

* ★ *

For Fay, Jeff, Barnaby, Bruno, and
Ziggy—my home away from home.

* ★ *

The family—that dear octopus from whose tentacles we never quite escape, nor, in our inmost hearts, ever quite wish to.

—Dodie Smith

THE HOUSE SWAP

PART ONE

HOME

CHAPTER ONE

ALLIE
IS AT CRINGLE COTTAGE, OXFORDSHIRE, ENGLAND

"I knew it! Middle child syndrome is officially a thing. I sent my parents an article about it that I found on the Good Parents Make Great Kids website. They haven't read it." (from my diary)

The fingerprint in the talcum powder I sprinkled on the handle of my desk drawer this morning proves it—someone has been going through my stuff. I read about the talcum powder technique in a book called *Think Like a Spy* that I found in the school library. Ms. Leonard said I could keep it for the summer, even though I already had the maximum number of books checked out. I take a picture with my phone and zoom in on the print, but I can't tell if it is a loop or a whorl. *Think Like a Spy* says that there are three main types of fingerprint patterns: the loop, the whorl, and the arch. I have an arch print—it's the rarest kind. Only 5 percent of the population has it, so the arch is the worst type of print to have if you are a criminal. I don't plan on being a criminal. I want to be a spy. I doubt having arch fingerprints is a barrier to becoming a spy.

My sister, Willow, has a loop print. I know that because I took her fingerprints last week. I suggested that we make a handprint painting of Chickpea, Nestle, and Nugget to decorate their henhouse. I could tell that Mum was surprised that I'd volunteered to do something with my little sister for a change—surprised and pleased because Willow is a lot of work. Willow pressed her palm onto a plate covered with white paint and pushed it down on a pale blue piece of paper to make the chicken's body; then she painted a yellow beak at the side of her thumbprint, added a red crest on the top of the thumbprint, and drew tiny eyes, legs, and feet with a black marker. She was very proud of it. The picture's not on the wall of the Chick-Inn yet because Willow's taking it around the village to show everyone, whether they want to see it or not.

I'm not sure how I'm going to get my brother's prints, but I'll think of something. It will be just my luck if Max has a loop print too. He probably does because it's the most common type. His prints will be much bigger than Willow's, though, so it should be easy to tell them apart. I took Mum's and Dad's prints too—they're both whorls. I wonder if you are more likely to marry someone who has the same fingerprint type as you. Maybe I should try to get Toby South's prints when we get back to school. How would I even do that? Imagine if he caught me trying to get his prints from his locker. I'd die. Even dogs have prints—not on their paws, though, on their noses. Bear didn't seem to mind me taking his nose print at all. I think he liked the taste of the food coloring I used to do it. He kept licking it off, so it took a long time to get a clear print.

I can't decide who the number one suspect for snooping around in my desk drawer is—Max or Willow. They both have reasons to go through my stuff. Max to find something he could use to embarrass or blackmail me with, like my diary—as if I'd ever risk keeping my diary in our house with a brother like him. And Willow because she is a thief, which my parents don't seem concerned about for some reason.

"Well, she didn't actually take anything," Dad said after I caught Willow trying to crack the combination lock on my money box.

"Only because she couldn't get it open! Why aren't you and Mum worried about this? Did you even read that article I gave you?"

After I found the calligraphy set that I got for my birthday under Willow's pillow a few weeks earlier, I printed out an article called "Is My Child a Kleptomaniac?"

from the Good Parents Make Great Kids website and presented it to my mum and dad.

"Actually, I did read it, and it said that it's a completely normal phase for a six-year-old," Dad said. "Relax. Also, did you sign me up for newsletters from that website? I keep getting random emails from them."

I don't think it's a completely normal phase, and I hate it when people tell me to relax. Maybe I could relax if my parents paid a bit more attention to what my brother and sister get up to. Maybe then I wouldn't have had to sign them up for the Good Parents Make Great Kids newsletter. Mum and Dad believe in free-range parenting, which is good for our chickens but not for my siblings.

As well as their generally casual approach to parenting, Mum and Dad didn't seem to give much thought to naming their kids. I guess Allegra is slightly better than Willow, but weirdly, the name suits her. I don't know what name would suit me, but it is definitely not Allegra. Fifty babies born in England last year were named Allegra, which is fifty too many, if you ask me. Thank goodness everyone calls me Allie. Well, everyone except Max, because he knows that I hate being called Allegra. I asked Mum what on earth they were thinking when they gave me that name.

"Allegra is a gorgeous name, Allie," she said, looking

offended. "It was always top of our list, wasn't it, Angus?"

I dread to think what else was on the list. Mum takes it really personally that I don't love my name, even though I'm the one who's stuck with it. I pointed out that she and Dad mostly call me Allie, except when they're annoyed with me and call me by my full name—Allegra Iris Greenwood—like when I won't play with my sister. I wonder if anyone ever got a restraining order against a six-year-old.

"Allegra's the name of an allergy medicine," Max said. "Side effects include being annoying, boring, and stupid."

"Actually, the name means 'joyful,'" Mum said.

Max snorted. I think I might be allergic to my brother, and there's no medicine for that.

"Anyway, Allie," Mum said, ignoring Max, "we wanted to give you a beautiful and unusual name. There were so many Emmas in my class that at least five people answered whenever the teacher said Emma, so I had to be called Emma V. Only one of us got to be just Emma, but she ended up being called Just Emma, so Emma V was probably better."

"Allegra is unusual," Dad said.

"Just not beautiful," Max said, smirking. "It really suits you, Allegra."

"Shut up, Maximilian Constantine," I said, which

wiped the annoying smirk off his face. He hates being called Maximilian, especially if I add his middle name.

"You shut up."

"You suck."

"You suck more."

I punched his arm. "Idiot."

He kicked my leg. "Loser."

Mum rolled her eyes. She always says that we'll grow out of our bickering eventually and become great friends.

We won't.

CHAPTER TWO

SAGE

IS AT CANYON VIEW, CALIFORNIA, USA

"Often called the heart stone, rose quartz is the crystal of unconditional love. Do you need to protect and grow the love around you? If so, this is the crystal for you." (from *Crystals A–Z*)

The guest rooms are just as perfect as they are each morning—the white comforters and pillows like freshly fallen snow. Nobody slept in here last night, that's for sure. I close the door behind me and exhale. Maybe I don't need to worry after all.

"Good morning, sweetie," Mom says, appearing from my parents' bedroom. "What are you doing in there?"

"Um, I heard Pandora meowing," I say, trying to ignore the fact that I can see Pandora delicately washing a white paw at the top of the stairs. "I thought she might have gotten shut in there. Oh, wait, there she is."

I point in Pandora's direction. Mom and the cat study me suspiciously.

I started checking the guest rooms a few months ago after my friend Nora told me that her dad sleeping in the guest room was when she and her brother knew for sure that their parents were getting divorced. I set my alarm clock for six every morning so I can check. I have no clue what I'd say if I did find one of them asleep in a guest room. Maybe I should stop checking bedrooms and just ask my parents what's going on. They always say I can talk to them about anything, but the words stick in my throat like a fish bone. Maybe I don't want to know the truth. Maybe I already do. Maybe if I ask what's wrong with them, just by saying the words aloud, by putting it out into the universe, I'll make it happen. So I don't.

Every day my parents act more and more polite around each other, and the more polite they get, the more worried I am. I miss their silly bickering, which always used to end in apologies, hugs, and often way too much kissing. Now they tiptoe around each other, and our house is as quiet as a library at midnight. I touch the white walls of the hallway, imagining the laughter that has soaked into them over the years. The quieter the house gets, the quieter I become. I wish for the thousandth time that I had a brother or sister to talk to about my parents—our parents. Somebody who would understand that when Mom and Dad are in the same room, even though they still smile at each other, it feels like someone has turned up the air-conditioning.

"You look very serious this morning," Mom says,

tucking my hair gently behind my ear. "How about some breakfast?"

"Is Dad up?"

"Not yet. He was working late last night. He'll probably sleep in."

"I can wait."

"Well, I can't—my stomach's growling. Come on, let's go eat," Mom says, steering me toward the stairs.

We always used to eat breakfast as a family on weekends. We'd make waffles, never pancakes, because Dad doesn't like them. We'd stack the waffles so high that they looked like the Leaning Tower of Pisa, top them with juicy blueberries, raspberries, and wafer-thin slices of banana, and then drench them with maple syrup. Dad explained that the Leaning Tower of Pisa doesn't fall over because its center of gravity is within the width of its base. He drew a diagram for me. Dad's an architect and is always teaching me interesting stuff like that. He says he thinks of everything in terms of shapes. When I was little, Dad used to describe our family as a perfect triangle with me balancing happily on the pinnacle and him and Mom smiling up at me from the bottom corners. Our triangle family was always an equilateral triangle in his drawings, but lately, we feel like a sad scalene triangle with all different angles.

When we get to the kitchen, Mom starts bustling

around, pulling eggs, berries, milk, and juice out of the fridge while I sit watching her, rubbing the rose quartz crystal I keep in my pocket with my thumb. It's a raw crystal, which means it's exactly the way it was when it came out of the ground—the edges haven't been smoothed and polished. The pale pink stone looks like a shard of ice, and you'd think the ridges would feel sharp and cold, but the crystal is smooth and warm. My friend Nora prefers the glossy tumbled stones, but there's something about the texture of this crystal that's comforting.

"Which one is it today?" Mom asks, smiling.

"Rose quartz," I say, holding up the crystal to show her.

"Pretty."

"It's called the heart stone. It's supposed to help with love and stuff."

Mom looks at me in surprise. "Is there someone you like at school you haven't told me about?"

"No!"

Mom smiles like she doesn't believe me. I don't tell her why I'm really carrying this particular crystal around, why it's the one I always have with me now, and why I've hidden small rose quartz crystals around the house, down the side of the sofa, and in their bedroom.

"Earth to Sage! Can I get some help here?"

"Why does Dad have to work all the time?" I ask, not moving.

"You know that he's really busy with that pitch for the hotel project in New York."

"Well, since I'm sleeping over at the twins' house after their party, maybe Dad could not work tonight, and you two could go out for dinner or to a movie or something."

"Maybe," she says, cracking an egg. She hands me the bowl and a fork. "Here you go. Whisk."

"It's been forever since you guys have been out, just the two of you."

I don't want to whisk. I want to tell Mom that if they went out and talked and laughed like they used to do, maybe our angles would be equal again. We might get back to being sixty degrees each.

"How about pancakes for a change?" Mom asks brightly.

"Dad hates pancakes."

"Dad's sleeping."

Suddenly, I'm not hungry.

CHAPTER THREE

ALLIE
WANTS TO GO

"If my brother wins another stupid trophy, I'm going to scream." (from my diary)

*T*hink *Like a Spy* says that I should be able to get a clear print from any object the person has touched firmly. I offered to clear Max's breakfast things this morning so that I could put his orange juice glass to one side for analysis later.

"What are you doing?" he asked, shoving my hand away as I reached for the glass.

"Clearing your stuff for you."

Max narrowed his eyes. "Why?"

"To be nice."

"You're never nice. I'll clear my own stuff."

So I am going with plan B, which is to get my brother's prints from his beloved computer. Max has got some big swim meet today, which means I'll have plenty of time to sneak into his room to get his fingerprints. I check I've got everything I need from the list in the book.

1. A tablespoon of cocoa powder. (I could only find hot chocolate, but it's pretty much the same thing.)
2. A small paintbrush. (All our paintbrushes have dried up because we never clean them properly, so I've taken one of Mum's makeup brushes. She won't notice. She hardly ever wears makeup.)
3. A piece of tape. (I eventually found some at the back of the "everything" drawer.)
4. A blank piece of card. (I'm using the back of an old Christmas card, also found in the "everything" drawer.)

"Bye, Mum!" Max shouts from the hallway.

"Good luck!" Mum yells back from the kitchen, where she's helping Willow learn how to "bake." I hope they don't need the hot chocolate.

"You don't need luck when you've got natural talent. Dad's going to have to put up another shelf for all my trophies," Max replies, banging the door behind him.

I count to one hundred before creeping into my brother's room with my equipment and the book. The directions seem very basic, but I guess it is a kids' book, so maybe they need to spell it out for the beginners. I wonder if there is a *Think Like an Advanced Spy.*

1. Dip the brush into the cocoa powder.
2. Use the brush to dust the item you are checking for fingerprints.
3. When you locate a clear print, tear off a piece of tape large enough to cover the entire fingerprint.
4. Carefully place the piece of tape on top of the print and press down.
5. Peel off the tape, place it onto the blank card, and push down firmly.

I press down the tape and study the print. Hurray! It's perfectly clear—even better than the chicken prints from Willow. A loop—I knew it. Now to remove all evidence of my investigation, which is one of the most important parts of being a spy, and one of the many reasons that, were I ever to decide to be a criminal, I would be much better at it than my brother or sister. I use a slightly damp tissue to carefully wipe down the keyboard and poke a cotton swab between the keys. Max will never know I was here. I think Phantom should be my spy name.

Mealtimes are always noisy and crowded at our house, but today it's even worse than usual. There is an

enormous gold trophy right in the middle of the table—
of course Max won again—and Willow's throwing a
party for her dolls, who are sitting around the trophy.
Her favorite doll, Ruthie, has a birthday party at least
once a week. Willow insists we all wear party hats,
even Bear, because, well, she's Willow. It's easier to just
go along with her. I tug at the elastic, which is cutting
into my chin, and scowl at my sister, who beams back
at me. Max doesn't seem to mind wearing a hat, even
though he looks like a complete idiot. He's laughing as
he watches Willow attempt to tie a large purple ribbon
around an apple, presumably Ruthie's birthday present.
It's not a mean laugh, though, and when he reaches over
to help her, I feel a burning sensation in my chest. I can't
remember the last time my brother did anything nice for
me. I look away.

Everyone's talking over each other as usual, and I
decide to see how long I can go without saying anything
before someone asks me what's wrong. I do this quite a
lot to see how much attention my family actually pays to
me. The answer is zero.

Max: "It's getting embarrassing that I keep winning."

Dad: "I guess I'll need to get that new shelf put up."

Willow: "Everyone has to sing 'Happy Birthday' to
Ruthie. She's turning ten today. Ready? One, two, three."

Everyone except me: "Happy birthday to you, happy birthday to you, happy birthday, dear Ruthie, happy birthday to you."

Max: "Coach says he'd put money on me making the National Junior Squad this year."

Willow: "Look! Ruthie got an apple for her birthday. That's her favorite."

Mum: "Lucky Ruthie. Angus, did you put any salt in the soup?"

Dad: "Can't remember. Anyway, I told Chris that he should talk to you about the bees."

Willow: "When I close my eyes, where do my eyeballs go?"

Mum: "Nowhere, darling. Angus, can you pass the salt?"

Max: "How cool is that? Olympics, here I come."

Dad: "Well done, Max."

Willow: "Can you see your eyeballs when your eyes are closed, Max?"

Bear: "Woof, woof."

Max: "Coach says I need more pool time, though, so—"

Mum bangs on the table. "Pool! That reminds me. Dad and I have some exciting news."

"What?" Max asks, spraying sandwich crumbs out of his mouth across the table, right in my direction. He definitely did that on purpose.

"I have exciting news too," Willow says, "and it's probably more exciting than your news, Mummy, because Bear is pregnant! He's going to have an actual baby."

Max starts choking on his sandwich, and Mum whacks him on the back. Unfortunately, my brother appears to be still breathing.

"I highly doubt *he* is pregnant," Mum says.

"You should check his tummy because he definitely, definitely is. Bear threw up in the garden again this morning, and Finn's mummy is always puking because she's going to have a baby. She barfs every morning, Finn says."

Willow makes some very realistic vomiting noises. Finn is my sister's best friend, who even my parents describe as a "handful." I have no idea why his parents decided to have another baby. Some people never learn.

"A puppy," Dad says.

Mum, Max, Willow, and I look at him.

"Bear would have a puppy, not a baby."

"Okay, Angus, let's not confuse matters further. Back to the exciting news—drumroll, please."

Willow, who is always up for making any type of noise, starts banging enthusiastically on the table with her knife and fork.

"Thank you, Willow. So, instead of going on holiday to

Cornwall as usual, this year we're going to California."

"Wow!" I say, forgetting that I'm not speaking.

"Yes!" Max says, high-fiving Willow. "Can I learn to surf while we're there?"

"That would be fun," Mum says. "I've always wanted to try surfing. The place where we're staying isn't far from the beach."

"I want to learn to surf too. Like in *Lilo & Stitch*," Willow says, jumping up and down. "I'll be Lilo."

That kid watches way too much television. I can't remember the last time I saw her with a book. She's never going to learn to read properly at this rate. Mum says not to worry and that just being around books is the most important thing. I could read by the time I was four. I must have been self-taught.

"I'll be great at surfing. Does Britain have a national surfing team?" Max asks.

I roll my eyes. "Surfing is lame. I'm not doing it."

"Course you're not, because you're scared," Max says.

I glare at him across the table.

"No, I'm not. I just don't like the beach."

That's the understatement of the year. I hate the beach—the sand gets everywhere, it's too hot, I always get sunburned—even when I wear factor one gazillion and one of those SPF shirts—and I'm scared of sharks, jellyfish, sea snakes, puffer fish, stingrays, stonefish, and most other things that live in the ocean. Plus, I'd be terrible at surfing. Why would I want to do something that I know will make me miserable and I will suck at? Maybe I'll be miserable because I suck, or maybe I'll suck because I'm miserable. I decide not to worry about it. I'm not doing it anyway.

"Is Bear coming?" Willow asks.

"Bear can't come to America," Dad says.

"But I don't want to miss Bear's baby being born, and I need him with me for when I go surfing. He's going to be Stitch."

"I guarantee Bear will not give birth while we're on holiday," Mum says, trying not to laugh.

"Disneyland is in California," Dad says. "You'll get to meet Elsa."

Willow's eyes light up. "The real Elsa?"

"The real Elsa."

Willow looks from Bear's stomach to Dad's face. "Okay. I'll come."

"Excellent. Delighted you'll be joining us."

"Where will we stay? Won't a hotel in California be expensive?" I ask. A horrible thought strikes me. "We're not camping, are we?"

The only thing worse than having to share a hotel room with my brother and sister would be having to sleep in a tent with them.

"No, we're not camping. We're doing a house swap with an American family," Mum says. "So we only have to pay for the flights, and they weren't too expensive because Dad booked us on some airline I've never heard of."

"Wait," says Max, "you mean a weird family is going to be staying here? Someone is going to be sleeping in my room? They had better not touch my computer."

My ears prick up. Surely my brother can't have noticed I was in there dusting his keyboard with hot chocolate. Maybe it was the smell. I should have thought of that.

Mum sighs. "They're not a weird family, and I'm sure they have absolutely no interest in touching your computer. Anyway, they have a daughter, so she may prefer to sleep in the girls' room. She's about your age, Allie. Her name's Sage, I think."

"Another stupid name," Max says. "You two have so much in common."

"Will I get my own room in California?" I ask, trying to pretend my brother doesn't exist.

"I don't see why not," Dad says. "The house has four bedrooms."

My own room. Bliss.

"But I want to share a room with you," Willow says, taking my hand in her small sweaty one. "Pleeeeeeease, Allie."

She bats her long, glossy eyelashes in a way that often convinces Mrs. Armstrong in the village shop to give her a free bar of chocolate. I'm immune to her eyelash fluttering.

"Nope."

"But I'll be scared without you, Allie," Willow says, changing her tactic to a trembling bottom lip.

"That sounds like a *you* problem," I tell her.

"We don't have to decide now," Dad says.

"We do, and it's decided. I'm having my own room."

"The house has a swimming pool, Max," Mum says as proudly as if she had installed it herself. "You'll be able to practice as much as you like."

"Ooooooh! A swimming pool," Willow says, thankfully distracted from the conversation about sleeping arrangements.

"If they have a pool and four bedrooms in California, why on earth do they want to stay here?" Max asks.

I don't often agree with my brother, but it's a valid question. Dad shrugs with a "beats me" expression on his face.

"Our house is lovely," Mum says, offended on the cottage's behalf, "and it looks charming on the Home Is Where the Heart Is website. Look." She grabs her laptop from the dresser, opens it, and shows us the listing for our house.

CRINGLE COTTAGE
OXFORDSHIRE, ENGLAND

Set in the heart of a handsome village in the stunning Cotswolds countryside, this charming and charac- terful three-bedroom seventeenth-century property comfortably sleeps six. A beloved family home, Cringle Cottage features a cozy sitting room with a flagstone floor and stone fireplace, a traditional cottage kitchen, and a delightful garden overlook- ing open countryside. Step back in time and enjoy an unforgettable family vacation at this very special home away from home.

I have to admit our cottage does look pretty, although I think "comfortably sleeps six" is false advertising. It isn't that comfortable with five. Where would the sixth person even sleep? In the bathtub? Oh well, it sounds like there are only three of them.

The photographs on the website have obviously been taken by someone standing on a chair in the corners of the rooms, as they look much bigger than they do in real life. So that's why my parents had a clearout a cou- ple of weeks ago. I should have known something was going on when Mum announced she was "decluttering" and ended up taking seven boxes to the charity shop in town. There's still plenty of junk around, though. When I opened the cupboard under the stairs yesterday, a pile of books, five board games, a tent, and two tennis rackets nearly crushed me.

"That sort of looks like our kitchen," Willow says, gazing around the room.

"Of course it does," Mum says. "It *is* our kitchen."

Willow studies her suspiciously.

"Are you sure, Mummy? I don't think so."

"I'm sure."

"The American family will probably sue you when they get here," Max says.

"Actually, they think the cottage looks adorable," Mum says. "The quintessential English cottage, the woman said in her email."

"Whatever," Max says. "Where are we going to stay, anyway? Is the house we're going to on this website?"

"No, but the owner sent me some pictures," Mum says, opening her email. "Isn't it amazing? We leave next week."

Max whistles, Willow gasps, and my jaw drops.

CHAPTER FOUR

SAGE
WANTS TO STAY

"Lapis lazuli is also known as the Wisdom Stone. It is the crystal of knowledge and truth. Do you need help revealing inner truths? If so, this is the crystal for you." (from *Crystals A–Z*)

Nora and Nico's parents live exactly one mile from school, in opposite directions. Today's birthday party is at their mom's house. Next week they'll have one at their dad's. We have a week one and a week two schedule at school, and the twins have a version of it at home. Week one is Mom-Mom-Dad-Dad-Dad-Mom-Mom, and week two is Dad-Dad-Mom-Mom-Mom-Dad-Dad. During the summer, the twins have entire weeks of just Dad or just Mom, but eventually, it all evens out. Fifty-fifty. At least they didn't take one twin each, like in that movie *The Parent Trap.* I once heard Mom tell Dad that Nora and Nico's parents' divorce was "ugly." Is there such a thing as a not-ugly divorce?

"Have fun and wish Nora and Nico happy birthday

from me," Mom says. She waits at the end of the driveway until Nora opens the door.

"Finally!" she says, pulling me into the house and handing me a red foam clown nose. "Here. Mom wants everyone to wear one. Just put it on for a second if you see her, then you can pretend you lost it. She's really overdone it this year. Come look."

Nora leads me through the house and out into the backyard. I wave to some kids from school and stop to pet Nora's dog, Pikachu, who is wearing a polka-dot ruffle around his neck and looking embarrassed. I'm a bit scared of dogs, especially big dogs, but Pikachu is a small, adorable, fluffy ball who I've known since he was a tiny puppy that could fit in the palm of my hand. Nora leans down, takes off Pikachu's ruffle, and hides it in a potted plant.

There are hay bales scattered across the lawn and red and white balloons tied to the fence. Carnival games are set up on the grass—there's a hoop toss, a paddling pool with rubber ducks floating in it with hooks on their heads, and a balloon blaster game. There's a photo booth with carnival-themed props and a cotton candy machine, and at the very end of the garden is a small red-and-white-striped tent with a sign reading Madame Zelda Knows All.

"Mom says our birthday parties are the best advertisement for her business," Nora says, rolling her eyes.

Nico appears at her side. "This is even worse than last year's theme," he says. "It looks like a little kids' party. Next year we're just going to the movies. No theme, no dressing up. Just salted popcorn with M&M's mixed in, a blue-raspberry Icee, and an Avengers movie."

"Sounds good to me," says Nora.

"I think it's kind of cool," I say, looking around the backyard. "And you have a photo booth, which is awesome. Happy birthday."

The twins are like two peas in a pod. They have the same favorite food, music, and TV shows, and they like the same sports. They both have gleaming black hair—Nora wears hers in two buns on the top of her head, like mouse ears, and Nico's is cut in a faux-hawk, super short on the sides and back and sticking up in the middle, which his mom hates, but I think looks cool. She says he looks like a cockatoo. Nora and Nico's mom calls us the Three Musketeers because we're always together. I wish I looked like them—then when we're out, people might think we're triplets. But we don't look anything alike. I'd love to have a sister or brother, even if they didn't look like me. I used to wish for a baby brother or sister every birthday when I was little. Even though I've got Nora and Nico and my other friends at school, sometimes "only" feels like lonely.

I hand them their gifts. I bought Nora a bracelet made of watermelon tourmaline. We started collecting crystals after a class trip to the Gem and Mineral Hall at the Natural History Museum. We bought our first ones in the gift shop. Nora says the gift shop is the best part of any museum.

"I love it! Watermelon tourmaline is so pretty," she says, giving me a big hug. "It's the friendship crystal, right?"

I nod.

"I'm going to get you exactly the same one for your birthday," she says.

Nico groans. "You two are so lame."

"Open yours," Nora tells him.

Nico rips off the turquoise-blue wrapping paper and pulls out a key ring with a mini-surfboard attached.

"Cool! Thanks, Sage."

He fist-bumps me instead of hugging. I can't remember when we stopped hugging or when he stopped dragging his mattress from his room into Nora's when I sleep over. I guess that's just what happens as you get older.

"Did you go see Madame Zelda yet, Nico? She told me that I'm going to win the US Open—singles, not doubles."

"You know that Madame Zelda is an intern from Mom's work, right?" Nico says.

"Are you sure?" Nora asks.

"Whoever she is, she's lame. The only reason I'd go see her is because Zane said she's giving out chocolate coins. I'm going to go get more cotton candy. Coming?"

"Want to get cotton candy too?" Nora asks, hooking her arm through mine.

"I'm not hungry. We had pancakes for breakfast," I say, feeling miserable all over again.

Nobody outside of my little triangle family would understand why pancakes for breakfast could make me sad—not even my best friend.

"Let's get our fortunes told, then. Madame Zelda has got something way better than chocolate coins in the goody bags. You'll love it," Nora says, pulling me in the direction of the tent.

We're almost there when she elbows me in the ribs.

"Shoot! Here comes Mom! Quick, put your clown nose on."

"Hi, honey. Hi, Sage. Are you having fun? Let me get a picture of the two of you for the Party Posse Instagram. I keep trying to get a photo of Nico, but he's lost his nose again."

Nora and I put our arms around each other and grin

at the camera while Nora's mom takes about a gazillion pictures of us.

"Beautiful," her mom says. "Are you excited about your trip, Sage?"

"What trip?" I ask. Nobody told me anything about a trip.

"Your mom mentioned you guys are going away."

"She did?"

Nora's mom flushes. "Um, I think that's what she said. I hope it wasn't supposed to be a surprise."

A surprise vacation? Maybe it's a surprise for Dad too. Maybe Mom has planned a big trip for his birthday. Maybe we'll go to Hawaii like we did for Mom's birthday a few years ago. We went surfing and collected shells on the beach and wore leis at dinner. I close my eyes and make a silent wish for leis, hand-holding, and laughter.

"Anyway, see you later, Mom," Nora says, tugging on my arm. "We're going to get our fortunes told. Come on, Sage."

Inside the tiny tent, it takes a while for my eyes to adjust to the dim light. Nora gives me a gentle shove forward. Madame Zelda is sitting at a small table with a red-and-gold scarf covering her hair. She's wearing a long, flowy dress and so many bracelets that she jangles when she moves her arms.

"Welcome," she says in a deep voice. She sounds like she just woke up or has strep throat.

"Hi, me again," says Nora. "My friend wants her fortune told."

"Hello," Madame Zelda says. "I remember you—the tennis player."

"Yeah. By the way, if my brother comes to see you, can you tell him his twin sister will win the US Open?"

Madame Zelda smiles and beckons me over.

"Come. Let's see what your future holds."

I sit down at the small table and watch as Madame Zelda rests her hands on a large purple cloudy glass ball and gazes at it intently. Nora nudges my shoulder, and I try not to giggle.

"You will be going on a long, long journey," Madame Zelda says in her sleepy voice.

"Mom was right," Nora whispers loudly. "You're going on vacation."

Madame Zelda shushes her and turns back to me. "This is no ordinary journey. You will travel to a mysterious land across the ocean. You must be courageous."

"Courageous?" Nora says. "Maybe you're climbing Everest."

The fortune-teller frowns at Nora and then stares at me so intently it makes me squirm in my seat. "To get what you want, you must act, not ask."

"What do you mean, 'act, not ask'?" I say.

"Like in a play? Oooh, maybe you're going to be in a movie, Sage," Nora says.

"No, no," says Madame Zelda, sounding impatient. "Not that kind of acting. I mean, your friend must take control of her destiny. She must be the star of her own story. Do you understand?"

"Nope," Nora says. "Do you, Sage?"

I shake my head. I have no idea what Madame Zelda's talking about.

"And remember, what you think you want may not be what you need."

Madame Zelda closes her eyes, and Nora and I look at each other. Is this part of the fortune-telling act, or did she go to sleep? It is really hot in here. Suddenly, she opens her eyes, smiles, and says in a wide-awake, non-strep-throat-y voice, "Anyway, time's up. Here's your goody bag. Bye, Nora. Goodbye, Sage. Next!"

"How do you think she knew our names?" I ask when we emerge from the tent, blinking in the bright sunlight.

"I just called you Sage like two minutes ago, and according to Nico, Madame Zelda is an intern at Party

Posse, so she's bound to know who I am. Mine and Nico's last ten birthday parties are all on the website. Anyway, open your goody bag. They're really cool. I made them."

Inside the red-and-gold bag are a miniature Magic 8 Ball, some large gold chocolate coins, and a tiny crystal.

"Which one did you get?" Nora asks, leaning over to look. "Oh, lapis lazuli. I love that one. Do you already have it?"

I shake my head. "Do you remember what it's for?"

"No, but we can check in the *Crystals A–Z* book later. I wish we could do our project on crystals instead of this dumb assignment. It's just our luck to have Ms. Klein again next year! Have you started yours yet?"

Our social studies teacher gave us a project called Family Takes Many Forms. She said we could create anything we like to do with family—a painting, a memory box, a story, or an interview with a family member. The project could even be about a family pet.

"The only rule is that at least five hours of work goes into this assignment, and believe me, I'll be able to tell if it hasn't," Ms. Klein said on the last day of school. "I don't want any last-minute efforts."

"Yeah. I'm doing my family tree," I tell Nora. "My grandma's been researching our relatives from England.

I'm kind of excited about it."

"Ugh! I'm not. If you feel like doing mine when you're done, you're welcome to. Nico and I are doing a joint project on being twins. I wanted to make a model of Pikachu, but Mom said that being twins is our thing. I bet I end up having to do all the work."

I laugh and Nora pulls me in the direction of the photo booth. Maybe I should tell her what my other summer project is—reminding my parents how much they still love each other.

The photo booth is crowded with friends from school, mostly girls, and we take lots of pictures of us holding up props on sticks: clown hair, clown smiles, ringmasters' hats, bow ties, black twirly mustaches, and balloons. Nora and I are laughing so much that tears run down our cheeks, and I decide not to say anything today. She probably doesn't want to think about parents and their divorces on her birthday.

I look for Madame Zelda later, but there's no sign of her. Either she isn't an intern for Party Posse after all, or she looks completely different without her fortune-teller costume on, or Nora and Nico's mom let her go home early since she made her spend three hours sitting in a stuffy tent. The "what you think you want may not be what you need" thing she said was weird. So was the "be the star of her own story." Nico said that Madame Zelda's a phony, but there was something about the way she looked at me, as if she could see right into my thoughts, that made me feel strange.

When Nora and Nico's mom drops me home on Sunday morning, Mom and Dad are in the kitchen drinking coffee. It's been a while since I've seen the two of them sitting at the table together without me. I decide this is a good sign.

"How was the party?" Dad asks.

"Good. It was a carnival theme. There was a fortune-teller and everything."

Mom laughs. "Kristen told me she was having some poor intern from Party Posse dress up as the fortune-teller."

So she *was* an intern. I feel silly now for thinking Madame Zelda might have been a real fortune-teller.

"There was a crystal in the goody bag." I hold out the stone to show my parents.

"Cool," Mom says. "What kind of crystal is it?"

"Lapis lazuli. Where did you guys go for dinner?"

"What?" Mom asks.

"I thought you were going out to dinner last night," I say, frowning.

"Who said we were going out?" Dad asks.

I look between the two of them, and then I realize that nobody had said it. I had suggested it.

"Anyway," Mom says, shaking her head a little. "We wanted to chat with you about plans for the summer."

So the twins' mom and Madame Zelda were right— we are going on vacation. I settle back in my chair to hear about the trip. I bet it's Hawaii. Hawaii would be good. Hawaii would be great!

"As Dad has got to be in New York for a few weeks with work, I thought it might be fun if you and I went on vacation—just the two of us."

Just the two of us? Without Dad?

"Why don't we all go to New York?" I ask.

"I thought it would be fun to go somewhere different," Mom says, smiling.

"I'll miss Dad," I say. I don't care that I sound like a baby. This is the worst time for my parents to be apart.

"You can FaceTime him whenever you like," Mom says.

I notice that she says, "*you* can FaceTime him," not "*we* can FaceTime him."

"Don't you want to know where we're going?" she asks, opening her laptop. "Drumroll, please."

Dad taps the table with his fingers.

"England!" she says. "You can do research for your summer project while we're there. You know how Grandma traced your great-great-grandmother Violet to the Cotswolds? I thought it would be the perfect place to visit."

"England!" Not even in the same country. I look between Mom and Dad. They're both smiling at me like I should be really pleased. I wonder how long Mom's been planning this trip. It must be weeks. Maybe months. "Is Grandma coming with us?"

"No, sweetie. She's going on that cruise, remember?"

"Well, why don't we wait until Grandma and Dad can come." I turn to face him. "You like England, don't you?"

"Show Allie where you'll be staying," he says, not meeting my eye.

Mom opens her laptop.

"I thought it would be cool to stay in the actual village where Violet lived. There aren't any hotels there, but I found a cottage on a house swap website. Since our house will be empty anyway, we're doing a swap with the family who lives there. Look! Isn't it cute? It's called Cringle Cottage."

Mom turns her laptop to face me, and I study the pictures of a small honey-colored stone house with cotton-candy-pink roses climbing around the door. It has tiny windows and a chimney with puffs of smoke coming out of it. It looks like the grandmother's cottage from the cover of the *Little Red Riding Hood* book I had when I was younger. I scroll down and examine the rest of the photos. A view from one of the windows shows a patchwork of apple-green fields stretching into the distance. They're so green that they don't look real. Inside the cottage, the small rooms are packed with furniture, and paintings are crowded on the wallpapered walls. It is almost the exact opposite of our house, which has mostly bare white walls. Dad hates houses packed with stuff. He's a minimalist. Whoever owns this house is a maximalist to the max. I bet we wouldn't be going to stay at Cringle Cottage if Dad were coming with us.

"And the family that lives there will stay here?" I ask.

"Exactly," Mom says.

"It looks tiny."

"I'd call it cozy, not tiny. The family who lives there has three kids. There'll be plenty of room for just the two of us."

"So there'll be three kids living here?"

I look around the table, trying to imagine a strange family eating breakfast. I can't.

"Yes. They have a son and two daughters. One of the girls is around your age. Allegra, I think her name is. Isn't that a pretty name? Maybe she'd like to stay in your room."

"Why can't they use the guest rooms?"

I don't want a strange girl staying in my room. I have everything perfectly organized. The books on the shelves are in alphabetical order, the hangers in my closet all face the same way, and my sweaters and T-shirts are carefully folded like the displays in stores. Even my Polaroids pinned to a white cord with tiny little wooden pegs are organized by subject: family, friends, Pandora, vacations. Vacations with all three of us.

"The whole point of doing a house swap is that it's a home away from home. You can't tell people not to use certain rooms," Mom says. "It's like the anti-hotel."

I would prefer to stay in an actual hotel—ideally, one in New York so we could be with Dad.

"What about Pandora?" I ask.

"Pandora will stay here," she says, "The English family will take care of her. They have a dog that we're going to be looking after. Won't that be fun?"

"Mom, you don't even like dogs. You always said that we're cat people. Plus, Pandora hates strangers."

Why would Mom rent a house where we have to look after some dumb dog? Dogs jump up all the time and slobber all over you and try to lick your face. Cats don't do that. Cats mostly keep themselves to themselves, although I guess it would be nice if Pandora sat on my lap sometimes.

"We're not adopting the dog, Sage," Mom says, starting to sound annoyed. "I thought you'd be excited."

I look back and forth between Mom and Dad. So much for us having a family vacation and my parents remembering how much fun they have together. How the heck am I supposed to get them to realize they are still in love when they're on opposite sides of the world?

CHAPTER FIVE

ALLIE
IS PACKING

"If anyone ever reads this, I'll die of embarrassment. I should have written it in secret code, but that would have taken forever." (from my diary)

Getting ready to go on vacation could be fun if I didn't have to help Willow pack. I don't see why Max can't do it. I told Mum and Dad they were being sexist, and they said not to be ridiculous. Willow has one of those suitcases on wheels that she rides on while someone, usually me, pulls her. The suitcase has orange and black stripes, tiger ears, and a tail. When she's riding on it, she smiles sweetly then roars at other travelers, who invariably think she's adorable. They wouldn't think that if they had to pull her for miles through the airport.

"Just make sure she doesn't put anything in there that will get us stopped at customs or ruin everything in the suitcase," Mum says. "Remember the chocolate ice cream incident?"

How could I forget seeing our suitcase coming around the baggage carousel leaking melted ice cream? My parents found it hilarious. It was not.

"Hey, this is mine. I've been looking for it every-where," I tell Willow, pulling my favorite sweatshirt out of her bag.

Willow opens her eyes as widely as she can in a way that she thinks makes her look innocent. It doesn't.

"Mummy must have put it in there," she says.

"Yeah right! Just leave my stuff alone. Wait, is that cheese?" I ask, spotting an orangey-yellow block wrapped in cling film in the front pocket of her bag.

"Cheddar," she says, as if that is a good reason to have cheese in her bag. "It's the best cheese."

"Willow, you can't put cheese or any kind of food in your suitcase."

"How about pickles?"

"No!"

After I've thoroughly searched Willow's bag and removed the cheese, a large jar of pickles, and a loaded water pistol, I get on with my own packing. I don't have many clothes that fit me, mostly because I've grown a lot this year. I'm nearly as tall as Max. I only ever choose to stand next to him to annoy him. Maybe Mum and Dad will take me clothes shopping in Los Angeles. I grab a few books from the Leaning Tower of Books on my dresser, which looks ready to collapse. If I ever go to Pisa, I will not stand anywhere near that tower—I have no idea how it is still standing. Now I just need to get my diary from its hiding place, and I'm ready to go.

Outside the Chick-Inn, Nestle and Nugget are scratching around as usual. Mum says they do it to keep their nails short and for social interaction. Chickpea, who is my favorite, is inside the henhouse. She likes her me time. Given Nestle and Nugget's idea of fun is to scratch the ground, I don't blame her one bit. I poke my head in through the door and say hi to Chickpea, who clucks gently in response. She has one eye open and one eye closed, which makes it look like she's winking. Dr. Ted, the village vet, explained that chickens' left eyes are connected to the right side of the brain, and the left side of the brain controls the right eye—or something like that. Basically, however it works, chickens can be asleep and awake at the same time, which is very cool. That would be an excellent skill to have in my history class. I've tried—it doesn't work, and Mr. Deepak asked me if I needed glasses.

I reach up to grab my diary from its hiding place on the ledge above Chickpea's nesting box, but it's not there. I run my hand from one end of the ledge to the other and then search the henhouse from top to bottom. Where is it?

"Mum, Dad!"

Chickpea opens both eyes and stares at me in surprise as I scramble out of the henhouse, sprint across the garden, fling open the back door, and whirl into the kitchen like a red-faced, red-haired tornado.

"Max took my diary!" I yell, glaring at my brother.

"Max, did you take your sister's diary?" Dad asks, not even bothering to look up from the newspaper.

"Why would I want to take her stupid diary? It's not like Allegra has a life," Max says.

I scowl at him, and he smirks.

"Willow!" I yell up the stairs. "Get down here."

"Willow can't even read properly," Dad says. "What would she do with your diary?"

"I'll bet there's nothing interesting in there anyway. 'Dear diary,'" Max says in a high, squeaky voice, "'today, nothing interesting happened as usual, and nobody likes me. Love, Allegra.'"

My sister appears wide-eyed at the kitchen door. She's dressed in a pale pink leotard and tutu, bumblebee tights, red Wellington boots, and the tattered straw hat that Mum wears to do the gardening in the summer.

"Willow, did you take my diary?" I ask, fixing her with my best "tell me the truth or else" stare.

"No," she says, looking hurt.

I bend down so I can look her right in the eyes.

"Really?"

"I promise, Allie," she says.

"Well, I'm going to kill whoever took it," I say. "I mean it."

Max rolls his eyes. "You probably lost it."

"I didn't lose it. Mum, Dad, do something!"

"I can't read curly letters," Willow reminds us.

"And I didn't take your stupid diary," Max says.

I spin around to face my sister. "How do you know the writing's curly?"

"All big kids do curly writing," she says.

I look at my parents pleadingly.

"There's not much we can do," Mum says. "Max, Willow, we trust you to do the right thing. If either of you took your sister's diary, please put it back where you found it."

"You trust them to do the right thing?" I splutter. "Are you kidding me? Make them give it back now." I can feel treacherous tears prickling my eyeballs and try to swallow the lump in my throat.

"Exactly what do you suggest we do, Allie?" Dad asks in an annoyingly calm voice. "Your brother and sister say they didn't take your diary. How about I help you look for it after dinner."

"I don't need to look for it. Someone took it. And I don't want any dinner. I'm going to bed!"

I squeeze my hands into fists and stomp out of the

room, turning at the door to give them all a final furious stare.

Half an hour later, I'm majorly regretting my decision to announce that I didn't want dinner and was going to bed early. My dramatic exit from the kitchen seemed like the best way to show my parents how upset I am, but one of them was supposed to follow me upstairs, persuade me to come out of my room, and promise me that my brother and sister are both in a world of trouble. But nobody followed me upstairs, and now I'm in bed at seven o'clock, and I'm starving. My anger's bubbling away like Dad's beef stew, which has been cooking all day in the Crock-Pot. If you leave the Crock-Pot on the highest setting for long enough, the lid rattles, and the pot looks as if it might explode. That is exactly how I feel. My lid is rattling.

Even when I do prove which one of them took it, I bet they don't get into trouble. I can only remember one time when my brother got into a lot of trouble, and that was five years ago. He got into so much trouble that he cried because **ONE**, according to Mum, Max felt genuinely horrible about what he did even though **TWO**, I knew Max was only crying because he felt genuinely horrible about not getting any allowance for a month and **THREE**, because he had to clean the bathroom for weeks even though **FOUR**, he claimed to be allergic to the bathroom cleaner and **FIVE**, he said he never meant to tell Chloe Belton that I still wore Pull-Ups at night even though I was **SIX**, which **SEVEN**, even my parents didn't believe.

Of course, Chloe Belton then told everyone at school that I still wore Pull-Ups, and I got called Allie Pee-Pee-Pj's for the rest of the year. I hate Chloe Belton. I know she's only started being fake nice to me because she's got a crush on Max. Chloe Belton's fake nice is worse than most people's actual mean. I wish she didn't live next door. She's always hanging around in her garden giggling with her friends, probably hoping to see my brother. It's so annoying when I go to feed the chickens. I can't even talk to them when Chloe's outside.

I look at the clock by my bed. Ugh! Only five past seven. I'm going to have to go downstairs and get some food. I stomp down to the kitchen, followed by Bear, who, as usual, is the only member of the family who cares how I feel. Dad is there on his own. He's loading the dishwasher even though I'm pretty sure it is Max's turn.

"Hi, sweetie, did you decide you want some supper after all? We finished the stew, but I made you a sandwich," Dad says, "just in case you changed your mind."

Great. My stomach was all ready for beef stew, and now I only get a sandwich. You would have thought that my parents would have known I'd get hungry, and that stew is my favorite, and have saved me a bowl. I'm about to tell Dad I don't want a stupid sandwich, but my stomach is growling.

"Here you go," he says, putting a plate in front of me. "Cheese and tomato—your favorite."

I sigh, pull out the slices of tomato, and start eating miserably. I can't stand tomatoes in sandwiches. They make the bread go all soggy.

"Cheer up, love. Next time you have a cheese and tomato sandwich, we'll be in sunny California."

I'm about to tell him that I hate tomatoes for the hundredth time, but what's the point?

CHAPTER SIX

SAGE
IS ALSO PACKING

"Blue lace agate is a wonderful gemstone for transforming negative energy into positive energy. It is a soothing and calming crystal that helps in the strengthening of relationships. Do you need rebalance and healing in your home? If so, agate is the crystal for you." (from *Crystals A–Z*)

Mom is in full-on planning mode for the trip to England. Travel guides for Oxford and the Cotswolds appear, which she happily studies, marking the pages of all the things she thinks we should visit with brightly colored Post-its.

"We're going to have so much fun! Our first girls' trip."

"I wish Dad were coming with us," I say for the hundredth time.

"Hmmmmm. Oh, Sage, look at this photo of Blenheim Palace. Isn't it gorgeous? It's only half an hour away from Little Moleswood. I wonder if we should rent a car while we're there. It's where Winston Churchill was born. It says here that there are one hundred eighty-seven rooms. Imagine having to vacuum. I'm so excited about our trip. Show me the photo Grandma gave you again."

I hand her a small silver frame. Inside is a black-and-white photo of my great-great-grandparents—Violet and Charles Wright. They are grinning into the camera so widely that they look like they've just won the lottery. My great-great-grandmother is wearing a long dress and veil and holding a small bunch of flowers. My great-great-grandfather is wearing a uniform.

"Do you want to make a copy of it for your assignment?" Mom asks.

"Yes, please. I'm going to stick it between their names on the family tree."

I've been working on my project when I've not been hanging out with Nora and Nico. I've named my assignment "The Sage Tree." I bought the biggest white poster board I could find in the art supply store and drew an enormous tree in the center with branches for my relatives. I'm going to put any information I find out about them next to their names. The tree looks quite lopsided because Dad doesn't know anything about his family before his grandparents, not even their names, and his parents died before I was born. My name is on the trunk of the tree. I look a bit lonely down there. The family tree templates I found on the internet all had boxes for siblings. Maybe I should make it a family and friends tree—then I could put Nora and Nico in boxes on either side of me.

"I wonder if they were violets," Mom says, interrupting my thoughts and pointing at the bunch of flowers my great-great-grandmother is holding.

Looking at the smiling faces in the wedding picture gives me a great idea.

"Why don't we watch your wedding video this evening?"

Mom and Dad watch the video every year on their wedding anniversary, but I can't remember if they did this year or not. The video has a soundtrack of all their favorite songs from when they were dating. It's kind of cringey, but I still like watching it.

"Gosh, we don't have time for that, Sage. I haven't even started packing yet. I'm going up to do it now. Are you done?"

"Almost," I say as Mom hurries upstairs. I don't think she hears me.

"I mean, maybe if we'd made more time for each other," I hear Mom say as I'm about to open her bedroom door to tell her my packing is done. "Maybe then things would have been different."

I let go of the door handle and press my ear to the

door, holding my breath. Whoever she's talking to on the phone gives an annoyingly long response during which Mom says things like: "exactly," "it's just so hard," "I could never have imagined," and sighs a lot.

"Thank you so much, Kristen. I don't know how I'd get through this without you. I'll give you a call when we're in England."

So she's talking to Nora and Nico's mom. I creep away from the bedroom door. I'm not the kind of person who would ever listen at the door—at least I didn't used to be. I tiptoe back to my room, Pandora slinking after me.

"What am I going to do, Pandy?" I ask her, and she blinks at me.

I pick her up, slump down on my bed, and bury my face into her long white fur. She tolerates my hug for about five seconds before wriggling free.

"Whatever," I say as she jumps off the bed. Pandora sits down and watches me with a judgmental expression on her face. My cat would be the worst emotional support animal. "Fine," I tell her. "I'm calling Nora."

"Hey," Nora says.

"Is your mom home?"

"Yes, and she's driving me crazy. She keeps nagging me to get off my computer and get on with my project. I mean, it's my summer vacation. Summer homework should be illegal. Plus, surf camp starts next week. It's my last chance to laze around. Why do you want to know where my mom is anyway?"

"I think she was just talking to my mom on the phone."

"She's always talking to your mom these days. Mom says Nico and I have too much screen time, but she's on her phone constantly. Plus, I know she takes it into the bathroom even though we're banned from doing it because, according to her, cell phones have ten times as many germs on them as a toilet seat!"

"You didn't hear what they were talking about, did you?" I ask.

"No. I'm hiding in my bedroom. I told you, she's trying to make me go and 'live my best life.' I told her that I am living my best life. Why?"

"I think my mom was talking to your mom about my dad."

"What did she say?"

"She said, 'maybe if we'd made more time for each other . . . things would have been different.'"

Nora sighs. "That doesn't sound good, does it?"

"No. If your mom says anything about my parents, will you tell me?"

"Of course I will. It's going to be okay, Sage."

I don't tell her that nothing will be okay if my parents get divorced. That she has Nico, so she's okay. That I'm scared and on my own.

"Sage, are you okay?" Mom asks.

I hadn't heard her come into my room. It would be pretty funny if she had been listening at the door to me talking to Nora, just like I'd listened to her talking to Nora's mom.

"I'm fine," I say.

"You don't look fine." She sits down on the bed next to me. "What's wrong, sweetie?"

Something, maybe everything, definitely not nothing.

"Nothing. I'm going to miss Dad, that's all. Aren't you?"

"We'll only be gone for ten days. Have you finished packing?"

"Yes," I say, pointing to the open suitcase full of perfectly folded clothes, shoes in shoe bags, and toiletries neatly organized in Ziploc bags in case anything leaks.

I've chosen some crystals to take with me to England and hidden some rose quartz and a sardonyx crystal in the pocket of Dad's laptop bag. *Crystals A–Z* said sardonyx is the best crystal for happy marriages, so I bought two for five dollars at Completely Crystals. I'll put the other one under Mom's mattress when we get to England. I chose the other crystals to bring on vacation by closing my eyes and holding each stone in my hand. Skylar, who works at the crystal store, said that sometimes the crystals choose you.

"You could pack professionally," Mom says. "My bag looks like Pandora fought with a mountain lion in there. I should have asked you to do it for me. By the way, Kristen called. She said to tell you to have a great vacation."

"What else did you talk about?"

Mom studies me. "The usual stuff. Sage, are you sure everything's okay?"

"I just wish Dad was coming with us."

"Hmmm."

"Don't you?"

"The two of us are going to have so much fun. How about you get ready for bed? We've got an early start tomorrow."

"Can you ask Dad to come in and say good night?"

"He said he'll be up soon. Sleep well, honey. Just think, next time you go to bed, you'll be at Cringle Cottage."

Mom leans down and kisses me, clicks off the lamp, and heads into the hallway, Pandora padding along at her side. My eyes feel heavy with sleep or maybe sadness, but I fight to keep them open. I turn the light back on and sit up in bed, hugging my knees to my chest while I wait for my dad to arrive.

When he comes in, he sits down on the bed next to me and ruffles my hair.

"Are you excited about the trip?"

"I guess. I wish you were coming with us. I'll miss you."

"I'll miss you too, honey, but it's only for ten days. Maybe you and I could plan something fun for when you get back."

"With Mom? It's more fun with the three of us," I say. "Don't you think?"

"I think it's time for you to get to sleep," Dad says. "Big day tomorrow. Good night, Sage. I love you."

"Night, Dad. I love you."

The gaps in Dad's replies are as obvious as the ones I have in my teeth in my first-grade school picture. He closes the door softly behind him. I know one thing for sure—going to England is not going to help this situation, not one bit.

PART TWO

HOME AND AWAY

CHAPTER SEVEN

ALLIE
SHOULD BE LEAVING CRINGLE COTTAGE

"Bear is 100% the only member of my family who gets me." (from my diary)

The next morning, even though I'm still mad at my entire family, I have that fizzy feeling I get in my chest before something exciting is going to happen. I don't know which I'm looking forward to more—going to California or having my own room for ten days.

"Are you going to miss me, boy?" I say, kneeling down and bracing myself for Bear to jump up and wash my face enthusiastically, but he doesn't even wag his tail. He just lifts his head a little, then drops it back down on the floor as if it's too heavy for him to hold up, and closes his eyes.

"Mum, Dad! There's something wrong with Bear."

Dad appears at the bottom of the stairs. "Come on, Allie. The taxi's here."

"Bear's sick. Come and look at him."

Dad sighs and trudges up the stairs. "He looks fine

to me," he says, glancing at Bear from the top stair and then at his watch.

"Dad, you barely looked at him! Come here and look properly. His eyes are all glazed, and remember, Willow said she'd seen him throwing up."

"He did," Willow says, appearing behind Dad and peering around his legs with a very serious expression on her face. "Bear barfed everywhere."

"I thought I told you to wait downstairs, Willow," Dad says.

"What's going on?" Mum asks, appearing next to Dad.

Dad sighs. "For the love of—"

"—it's Bear," I say. "There's something seriously wrong with him."

"He looks okay to me," Max says, emerging from his room.

I don't think we've ever all stood on the landing before. There isn't enough space.

"For God's sake, can everyone please just go downstairs," Dad says. He looks as if he is about to lose it completely.

"You're right, Allie. He doesn't look well," Mum says, ignoring Dad and kneeling down next to me to take a closer look at Bear.

"He's pale," I say. "We can't just leave him with people we don't even know when he isn't well."

"Don't be stupid, Allegra," Max says. "A dog can't be pale."

"Well, he is, Maximilian," I say, "so shut up."

Bear groans miserably.

"Mum, we can't leave him like this. What if he dies while we're on holiday?" I say, hot tears filling my eyes.

I lift Bear's head and gently place it on my lap. He barfs frothy green liquid all over my jeans.

"Ugh, gross!" Max says, putting a hand over his nose and mouth. "I'm going to wait downstairs."

"Ooooh, it's green!" Willow says, leaning over to get a closer look.

"Max, tell the taxi driver we'll be there in a minute," Dad yells after my brother.

"Angus, we need to take the dog to the vet," Mum says.

Dad rubs his forehead. "For heaven's sake, can't we have a straightforward trip? Just once? We're going to miss the flight. We could ask Gwen Armstrong if she minds taking Bear to the vet."

"But what if there's something really wrong with him?" I say. "What if he dies?"

"He's not going to die," Dad says, looking at his watch again.

"It's not fair to expect Gwen to take on the responsibility of a sick dog," Mum says.

"Can't we just get a later flight?" I ask. "When we know that Bear's going to be okay."

"It costs a fortune to change flights," Dad says with a pained expression on his face.

Mum looks at Bear and then back at Dad. "Can you please just phone the airline, Angus? I'll call Dr. Ted. Allie, you go and change out of those jeans."

"I'm not leaving Bear," I say.

Dad sighs and stomps downstairs, followed by Mum. Willow joins me on the floor to watch over Bear. For once, I don't mind when she takes my hand in her small clammy one and gives it a little squeeze.

Fifteen minutes later, Dad has established that it will cost seventy-five pounds per person to change the flights—a fact that caused him to let out a string of curse words, much to Willow's delight. Mum has established that Dr. Ted is currently at the farm dealing with a Shetland pony with an inflamed hoof but that he should be back at his office in an hour at most.

"Right," Mum says. "Angus, you and the children head to the airport and catch the flight as planned; then we only have to change my ticket. I'll call you as soon as I know what's happening with Bear. Allie, why aren't you changed? Hurry up."

"I told you, I'm not leaving Bear," I say.

"I'm not going to America if Allie's not going," Willow says.

"You're both going," Mum says.

"I'm not," I say, "and you can't make me."

"Same," Willow says, letting go of my hand and folding her arms across her chest.

"We're supposed to be going to Disneyland on Friday," Dad says. "You don't want to miss that, do you? Remember, Elsa will be there."

Willow tilts her head to the side. "You mean I wouldn't get to see Elsa at all?"

"You wouldn't," Dad says, shaking his head sadly, "and Elsa was really looking forward to meeting you. She told me. She's only there for the rest of the week. Then she has to go back to wherever she lives—the snowy place."

"Arendelle," Willow says sadly, pats Bear and me, and heads for the stairs.

"Well, I couldn't care less about Elsa, and I'm not going anywhere until I know Bear's okay," I say, sticking my chin out and crossing my arms to make it clear to my parents that they will have to carry me and my green-barf-covered jeans into the taxi, through the airport, and onto the plane kicking and screaming if they try to make me leave my dog.

"Nobody's going anywhere at this rate," Dad says crossly, looking at his watch again. "We're all going to miss the flight. The plane leaves in four hours."

"How about this," Mum says. "You, Max, and Willow fly out today, and Allie and I will come as soon as we know what's happening with Bear."

"That's ridiculous," Dad says.

Mum nods in my direction and raises her eyebrows. "Any better ideas?"

My parents have a hissed conversation during which they look at me multiple times, until eventually Dad lets out a deep sigh, shrugs his shoulders, kisses Mum and me goodbye, and heads downstairs.

"Do you think we'll be able to bring Bear home tomorrow?" I ask Mum when we finally get back to the cottage.

"I hope so, love."

Dr. Ted said Bear needed surgery and had to stay at his office overnight. I asked him if I could sleep on the floor next to Bear, but Dr. Ted said no. I pointed out that when I had my appendix taken out last year, the doctors let Mum sleep in a pullout chair next to my bed, but Dr. Ted wouldn't change his mind.

The cottage is weirdly quiet. I can't remember the last time it was just Mum and me here—maybe it never was.

"What are we going to do when the house swap people get here?" I ask.

"Ugh! I'd completely forgotten about them. I'll text

Lauren now. I hope they aren't going to be too annoyed that we're still here."

"Where are they going to sleep?"

"I suppose I should put Lauren in my room. Sage can sleep in Max's room, and I'll come in with you."

"Poor Sage," I say. "We should at least spray air freshener in there."

"Good idea!" Mum says. "I'll open the window and light a scented candle as well. The other day when I was in there, I found half a salami sandwich under the bed. God knows how long it had been there."

I feel bad for the American girl. Imagine having to sleep in the bed Max snores and farts in every night. Gross.

The house swap people still haven't arrived by ten p.m., and I'm too exhausted to stay awake any longer, so I drag myself to bed. I curl up on my side, pull the covers over my head, squeeze my eyes tightly shut, and whisper, "Please let Bear be okay," over and over. I'll do anything if he can just be okay. I'll even try to stop fighting with Max and being impatient with Willow. Thinking about my brother and sister makes me think about my missing diary. I bet it was Max who took it. I wonder if he took it to America. I wonder if he's read it. Maybe he'll be reading it on the plane right now and laughing at me. Maybe he'll read it aloud to Dad and Willow, and they'll all laugh. Maybe Max will tell Toby South that I wrote in my diary that I like him. Maybe he already told him. It makes me feel like a snail without a shell even to think about it.

CHAPTER EIGHT

SAGE
IS ARRIVING AT CRINGLE COTTAGE

"The moonstone is a stone of new beginnings. Are you planning a fresh start? If so, this could be the gem for you." (from *Crystals A–Z*)

"This can't be it," I say, peering out of the taxi window at what looks like a hobbit house. I knew we should have stayed in a hotel.

"It did look bigger on the website," Mom says. "Still, it's adorable, and they left the lights on for us. That's so considerate of them."

The taxi driver helps carry our bags to the front door and looks as if he's going to hug Mom when she gives him a twenty-pound tip.

"Thanks, love," he says in a weird accent. "You Americans are always the best tippers. Naming no names, but I once got a pound tip for that same trip from someone in this village."

"You're welcome," Mom calls after him as he heads back through the small metal gate to his taxi. "Now, I wonder where they'll have left the key."

She rummages through her bag, looking for the instructions she printed out before we left home.

"It says here that the key is under the sheep statue, by the front door."

"Which sheep statue?" I ask. "There are six."

"Oh, I don't know, Sage, just have a look underneath them all," Mom says, sounding tired.

It does feel like a really long time since we left home and said goodbye to Dad at the airport. It felt all wrong for him to go to a different terminal to get his flight to New York. I kept hoping he'd appear on our plane, and we'd all laugh about the joke Mom and Dad had played on me by making me think he wasn't coming. There was even an empty seat in our row until right before the doors closed, when a lady came hurrying on and sat down in it, making my face fall, and my heart sink into my sneakers.

"It's under the smallest one. The one with the adorable face," says a clear voice from the door.

Mom and I both jump.

"Oops, sorry to scare you!"

"Did we get the wrong house?" Mom asks, looking confused. "Or the wrong day?"

"No, no. I'm Emma Greenwood, and this is Cringle Cottage. You're exactly where you're supposed to be at exactly the right time. It's me who isn't—well, we—Allie and me. Anyway, do come in, and I'll explain it all. We're still here because of poor old Bear. You must be Lauren and Sage. Didn't you get my message?"

"What message?" Mom asks, following Mrs. Greenwood through the low-framed doorway and into a tiny hall.

Mrs. Greenwood stops in her tracks and turns. "Oh dear. I did text you. The dog started barfing green stuff all over the place just as we were about to head to the airport this morning, and we couldn't leave him like that, so Allie and I, that's my eldest daughter, stayed here while Angus flew to Los Angeles with Max and Willow." She lets out an enormous breath. "Sorry, what a mess. Let me put the kettle on and we'll have a nice cup of tea. Come through."

Mrs. Greenwood leads us into a cozy kitchen, which is crowded with furniture. There's a striped armchair, a round table with six chairs, a big wooden dresser crammed with blue-and-white plates, dried flowers, little china sheep, and a small jungle of plants. On the table is three-quarters of a delicious-smelling cake, a bottle of red wine, and a green-and-white-patterned jug overflowing with pink and lilac flowers. There's a drawing of a house, five stick figures, a horse that is almost as big as the house, and the word *WELLCOM* scrawled across the top of the paper in gigantic multicolored letters.

"Willow drew that for you," Mrs. Greenwood says, smiling fondly at the drawing. "She's my youngest. Awful, isn't it? You can't even tell that's supposed to be a dog. It looks more like a horse to me."

Mom looks horrified. Every drawing I ever did, however bad, was pronounced a work of art and stuck on the fridge. She even kept my old finger paintings from preschool.

"Don't worry," Mrs. Greenwood says, "she can't hear me. Willow is at your house. At least, they should have arrived by now, I think. I can't work out the time zones, and Angus hasn't phoned yet. It's just Allegra and me here. Allie. For God's sake, don't call her Allegra. She can't stand her name, poor thing. Anyway, she's asleep. She was exhausted after the whole drama with Bear."

"Who?" Mom asks.

"Bear, the dog."

"Where's your dog now, Mrs. Greenwood?" I ask, looking around the kitchen. I'm struggling to follow the conversation. Mrs. Greenwood bounces from one topic to another. It's making my head spin.

"Please, call me Emma, dear. 'Mrs. Greenwood' makes me feel like my mother-in-law, and she's dreadful. Bear is staying at the vet's surgery. We're terribly worried. Apparently, he's been throwing up a lot recently—Bear, not the vet. Willow says he's pregnant. I'm talking about the dog again, not Dr. Ted. Ha ha!"

Mom and I exchange glances. I can tell Mrs. Greenwood is making her dizzy too.

"Well, what are we supposed to do now?" Mom asks, sounding exhausted. "Is there a hotel nearby?"

"Goodness, no, I wouldn't dream of it. You'll be in my room, Lauren. Sage, you'll be in Max's room. It was a bit smelly in there earlier—you know what teenage boys are like. I lit a lovely scented candle and opened the window for you, so it should be fine now. I'll sleep with Allie in her and Willow's room."

"I think we'd be more comfortable in a hotel," Mom says. She is starting to look annoyed as well as tired.

"No, no. There's plenty of space for all of us here, Lauren," Mrs. Greenwood says, waving her arms around as if she's demonstrating just how much space there is and almost knocking over the jug of flowers in the process. "Anyway, the nearest hotel is about half an hour away, and by the time we get you a taxi to take you there, it will be the middle of the night."

Mom looks at me and shrugs. "It doesn't seem like we have much choice, does it? We can figure something out in the morning."

"Excellent," Mrs. Greenwood says. "I'm so glad you don't mind. Allie seemed to think you might be annoyed we were still here."

I look at Mom and raise my eyebrows, hoping she picks up on my "I told you we should have stayed in a hotel all along" vibes. I think she does.

Mrs. Greenwood takes us on a tour of the downstairs of the cottage, which takes about sixty seconds since there is only the kitchen, a small living room, and a tiny bathroom, or "downstairs loo," as she calls it. Then she starts telling us all about her dog's green vomit. I try and fail to hide a yawn so enormous that it makes my jaw click.

"Gosh," Mrs. Greenwood says. "How rude of me. You must be absolutely exhausted, you poor thing. Let me show you to your rooms. I put some fresh towels at the ends of the beds. Just let me know if there's anything else you need."

The room where I'll be sleeping is small, with a sloping roof. A single bed is tucked against the wall where the ceiling's lowest side is. I wonder how the boy who lives here—Max, I think his mom said his name is—manages not to bump his head when he gets out of bed. The sheets are red and white striped. Mom sniffed them when Mrs. Greenwood finally left the room and pronounced them clean. The room itself smells of roses and freshly cut grass, which seems strange for a teenage boy. I guess it must be the scented candle and the open window. There's a small desk and a large computer with a *DO NOT TOUCH!!!* sign taped to the screen. I understand the boy not wanting people to touch his stuff, but it was rude of him to leave a sign. I think of my sign-free bedroom with its crisp white sheets and sigh. I hope nobody is sleeping in there, especially not this boy. At least we'll be in a hotel tomorrow night.

CHAPTER NINE

ALLIE
IS STILL AT CRINGLE COTTAGE

"Mum and Dad didn't believe me when I told them Max had put my toothbrush down the loo." (from my diary)

When I go to the bathroom the next morning, I see two very fancy-looking toilet bags. One is cream leather and has initials monogrammed on it in navy-blue letters so swirly I can't even read them, and the other is pale pink with *BELIEVE* printed on it in silver letters. Believe what? The toilet bags are sitting neatly on the shelf alongside two electric toothbrushes, which look totally out of place next to the mug containing seven toothbrushes with chewed-looking bristles owned by various members of my family. Who on earth do they all belong to? Dad, Max, and Willow must all have theirs with them. I started keeping my toothbrush in my bedroom after I went in to brush my teeth one evening and the bristles were soaking wet. Max probably put it in the toilet, or maybe he brushed Bear's teeth with it. I hope it was Bear's teeth.

I'm tempted to peek inside the toilet bags, but I resist in case the owners notice someone has been rummaging through their stuff. Who knows, they may have read *Think Like a Spy* as well. The presence of the fancy toilet bags and high-tech toothbrushes, plus the fact that Mum was asleep in Willow's bed when I woke up, mean that the American people must have arrived. I wonder what they said about us still being here. I bet they were not happy.

Downstairs on the kitchen table is an empty wineglass, half a cup of juice, an empty water glass, and half of Mrs. Armstrong's secret recipe ginger cake. I pick up a crumb and pop it into my mouth. The moist, spicy deliciousness makes my tongue tingle, and I decide a slice won't be missed. Mum says cake is just an oversize muffin, and muffins are 100 percent breakfast foods. I stretch out on the sofa with an enormous slice. Blissful silence. No noisy footsteps coming from upstairs. Despite being small, Willow sounds like a baby elephant when she's running around up there. No Max being annoying. If only Bear were here, this would be the perfect start to my day.

"Um, hi?"

I look over to see a girl standing at the bottom of the stairs. I didn't even hear her come down. Mum said she's eleven like me, but she looks older. Also, since when is "hi" a question?

"Hi," I say, followed by a firm full stop.

I study the girl, who's looking at me shyly. She has fine, wispy sunshine-colored hair in two fancy braids that reach halfway down her back, very round, very blue eyes, pale eyebrows and eyelashes, and a heart-shaped face. It's important to notice face shapes when you describe someone—hair color, eye color, and even your nose can easily be changed, but changing your face shape is almost impossible. If I ever witness a crime, the police will be very impressed when I include the face shape in the suspect's description. My face is diamond-shaped. There are seven different face shapes: oval, round, rectangular, square, heart, triangle, and diamond. Disney princesses always have heart-shaped faces, and this girl reminds me a lot of Elsa from *Frozen*. Willow would be obsessed.

She's dressed in denim shorts and a pale pink hoodie with *LOVE* written on it in silver letters, probably bought from the same shop where she got the *BELIEVE* toilet bag. Who gets dressed before breakfast? Nobody in my family does. I'd probably spill orange juice down my front and have to go and get changed again. She has a pale pink heart-shaped crystal on a silver necklace that she keeps touching. The girl's fingernails are painted silver. She's wearing socks, so I can't tell if her toenails are painted silver too. I bet they are. I look down at my own bitten fingernails, toenails that need cutting, and very uncool purple polka-dot pajamas, which don't even fit me. Last night Mum dug them out of the pile of clothes that are waiting for Willow to grow into. I do have nicer pajamas, but they're in my suitcase, and Mum said there was no point unpacking.

The girl's blue-blue eyes look a bit red, which I suppose must be because she's jet-lagged. Maybe she's been crying, but why should she cry? Unless it's from sleeping in Max's room, in which case I wouldn't blame her.

CHAPTER TEN

SAGE
IS ALSO AT CRINGLE COTTAGE

"Carnelian is a stone that promotes confidence and creativity. Are you faced with a new situation and need to overcome feelings of shyness? If so, this could be the gem for you." (from *Crystals A–Z*)

The English girl has red hair cut in an uneven bob, which looks like she cut it herself without even watching a YouTube video first, and pale, freckly skin. I've never seen so many freckles on one face. I hope she has some super strong sunscreen for when she gets to California. If she ever gets there. She's studying me with her head tilted slightly to one side. Her eyes are a warm chocolate-brown color. She reminds me of a red squirrel. She's wearing cozy-looking yellow-and-purple polka-dot pajamas. I shiver—if this is summer in England, then I'm going to need some warmer clothes.

"Sorry we're still here," she says, not sounding sorry at all. "And sorry you had to sleep in my brother's room." She does sound sorry about that.

"It's fine," I say, in an "it's not really fine, but I'm too polite to say anything about it" voice. "How's your dog?"

The girl scrunches up her freckled nose. "I don't know. We're going to go to the vet's office as soon as it opens. Dr. Ted said Bear will be fine, but it's not like he's going to tell us if he thinks our dog might be about to die, is he?"

"I guess not."

We stand there staring at each other.

"Um, I have a cat," I say to fill the silence. I hate it when nobody speaks. It feels super awkward. If nobody answers a question in class, I always feel like I have to, like it's mean to the teacher if nobody does. "She's called Pandora."

"I don't like cats."

How rude. I don't like dogs, but it's not as if I'm going to mention it, especially since her dog is sick right now.

"Well," I say, "Pandora doesn't like people, so you guys will get along just fine."

The girl bursts out into a shout of laughter that fills the room. It's the kind of laugh that makes you want to laugh too.

"I don't like people much either, especially my brother," she says. "I'm Allie, by the way."

"I'm Sage."

"Wow, your name is as bad as mine. How about some cake? We can eat it in the garden, and I'll introduce you to Chickpea, Nestle, and Nugget."

"Who are Chickpea, Nestle, and Nugget?" I ask.

"The chickens. Who else would be in the garden called Chickpea, Nestle, and Nugget?"

"You have chickens?"

I'm 99 percent sure Mom did not know there are chickens here.

"Yup. And bees, but they don't have names, except for the queen, of course—she's called Beeyoncé. Get it?"

Mom definitely did not know about the bees! I stand and watch as Allie hurries toward the back door of the cottage. Meeting a trio of chickens and a bee named Beeyoncé was not how I expected to spend my first morning in England.

"Come on!" she yells over her shoulder, and I follow her nervously.

CHAPTER ELEVEN

ALLIE
IS PRICKLY

"Nothing interesting ever happens in Little Moleswood. Nothing." (from my diary)

A woman with the same sunshine-blond hair, round blue eyes, and heart-shaped face as Sage appears in the garden just as we are finishing our ginger cake—Sage her first slice and me my second. She's wearing white jeans, a flowy pale blue top, a pair of dangly gold earrings shaped like palm trees, and shimmery lip gloss. I don't know why she's so dressed up. It's not like there's anywhere to go in Little Moleswood.

"There you are," she says, sounding relieved.

She makes it sound like she has been looking for Sage for hours, but it only takes three minutes to search our entire house and garden, including looking under the beds and in closets. I know because I've timed it.

Sage's mum looks less like a mum and more like an older sister or cousin. She even has a young voice—like pink lemonade.

"Hi, you must be Allie. I'm Lauren."

Is it just me, or does it always feel super awkward to call people's parents by their first names? I can't remember Sage's last name, though, so I guess I will just have to avoid calling her mum anything.

My own mother appears in the doorway behind Sage's mum, yawning, earringless, glossless, and wearing an ancient tartan dressing gown of Dad's, which has definitely seen better days. My mum looks very mum-like compared to Sage's mum, and I decide this is a good thing.

"Good morning. How did everyone sleep?" Mum asks.

"Surprisingly well," Sage's mum says, which I think sounds a bit rude.

"I see Allie helped you find some breakfast," Mum says, giving Sage one of her broad smiles that crinkle up her eyes. "How about you, Lauren? What would you like for breakfast? There might even be some cake left."

"Maybe just some granola and fruit, if you have it," Sage's mum says. "Do you have almond milk?"

"Sorry, we only have boring old cow's milk, Cheerios, and we definitely have bananas," Mum says. "Does that work for you?"

Sage's mum does not look as if Cheerios, bananas, and boring milk work for her.

"Perhaps just coffee. I can get it if you show me how to use the coffee maker," she says.

Mum laughs. "If you know how to boil a kettle, you know how to make coffee in this house. I'll show you where to find everything. Come on, Allie, we need to go and see how Bear's doing. Let's make ourselves present-able. I don't want to terrify Dr. Ted."

Twenty minutes later, Mum is looking at Dr. Ted incredulously.

"Did you say bloat? Gas? Wind? Oh my god! Angus is going to be furious. It cost one hundred and fifty pounds to change the flights."

"It's a lot more serious than wind, Emma," Dr. Ted says sternly. "Left untreated, Bear could have died. The official name is gastric dilatation-volvulus."

"Is he going to be okay, Dr. Ted?" I ask, scowling at Mum.

Who cares about money when Bear's life is on the line? Mum always says money can't buy happiness, but in this case, it did, because we wouldn't be able to pay the vet's bills if we didn't have enough money.

"The surgery went extremely well. Bear should be feeling like himself in no time. Big dogs like him are more at risk of GDV due to their increased thoracic height—to-weight ratio," Dr. Ted says.

"Their what-to-what ratio?" Mum asks.

"Basically, Bear has a deep chest. Do you want to

come and see him? He's still a bit woozy from the anesthetic."

Mum and I follow Dr. Ted into the room where the animals that have to stay overnight sleep. The current residents are Bear; the vicar's guinea pig, Queenie; and a baby hedgehog that Mrs. Armstrong found injured outside her shop last week. I'm not sure if the hedgehog has a name yet, but I'm going to suggest she call her Holly Berry. I wonder if Mrs. Armstrong plans to keep Holly Berry. If not, I'm going to ask Dr. Ted if I can have her when Mum isn't listening. She can live in the garden. Mum will never know.

Bear is lying on his favorite pale blue fluffy blanket, which we brought in from home yesterday. He is snoring noisily, his big chest rising and falling. A patch of his tummy has been shaved, and there is a large white square bandage covering part of it. He's not twitching like he often does when he's asleep. Mum always says he's dreaming about chasing rabbits when he does that. I guess he doesn't feel like chasing rabbits after his operation.

"Hey, boy," I say, kneeling down to place a gentle kiss on his silky forehead. He smells of disinfectant and metal instead of his usual aroma of grass, honey, sunshine, and dog food. "I missed you."

"He looks good. Doesn't he, Allie?" Mum says, kneeling

next to me and placing her hand on Bear's chest. "Who cares what your dad says about the money. Bear is priceless."

"We'll need to keep him in for another day or two," Dr. Ted says. "Are you still planning on going on holiday?"

"I don't know," Mum says. "I mean, we'd like to, but we wanted to wait and see what was happening with Bear before we decided anything. What do you think?"

"Well, as long as you have someone who can keep a close eye on him, then I think it's fine for you to go. Don't you have guests staying at Cringle Cottage? Can they take care of him? They'll need to bring him to see me in about a week so that I can take the stitches out, but apart from that, all he needs is plenty of rest."

"And love," I say. "He'll need plenty of love, and I don't think Sage and her mum are dog people."

"I'll talk to Lauren about it," Mum says, "but I would completely understand if she doesn't feel comfortable taking care of Bear. It's one thing to look after someone else's pet, but it's quite another to look after an animal who has been ill, even if it was just gas."

Dr. Ted and I both glare at Mum.

"It was gas?" Sage's mum says when we get home, her pink-lemonade voice bubbling with laughter.

"Actually," I say, scowling at her, "the medical name

is gastro-dilution-volvo, or something like that, and Dr. Ted said it is extremely serious. Bear could have died. And Dr. Ted never exaggerates."

"Well, thank goodness he's going to be okay," she says, and turns to Mum. "Um, Emma, I hate to ask, but just so we can make our plans, do you have any idea if or when you might be leaving? Maybe it would be better if Sage and I checked into a hotel. I looked online, and it said there's a bed-and-breakfast in the next village."

"Oh, no," Mum says. "You don't want to stay there. Gwen Armstrong, who owns the village shop, said that Joyce, who does the flowers in the church, told her that her brother Lewis, who lives in Canada, I think he might be an accountant, said he is sure that he and his wife got bitten by bedbugs when they stayed there last Christmas."

Sage's mum shudders.

"Anyway, please don't feel you need to move out. It's us who shouldn't be here. We'd much rather you stay, wouldn't we, Allie? We would still like to go to California if possible, providing Bear is okay. Dr. Ted said he should be fine, but I'd completely understand if you don't want to look after him."

"What would we need to do?" Sage's mum asks, looking nervous. "We're not really dog people. I mean, we like them, but we've never had one, have we, Sage?"

I give Mum an "I told you they aren't dog people" look, but she studiously ignores me.

"Apart from the usual stuff—food, water, rest, and lots of hugs—he'll need to have his stitches taken out in a week."

Sage's mum looks at Sage and then back at Mum and takes a deep breath.

"I'm sure we can manage," she says. "We'll take good care of him, and if he seems even a little bit sick, we'll call the vet."

Mum practically does a dance on the spot and hugs Sage's mum.

"If you're absolutely sure it's okay with you, I'll rebook the flights, maybe for a couple of days from now, so we can make sure Bear is settled in before we leave. I'm so excited. I honestly didn't think we'd make it to California. Thank you, Lauren. You're a lifesaver—well, a vacation saver!"

"You're welcome. By the way: I don't feel comfortable taking over your room while you're still here. Why don't I move into your son's room for a few days, and the girls can share Allie's room? I haven't unpacked yet, so it's no problem."

Mum looks delighted. She was complaining this morning that her back is in agony from the bunk bed. How does she think I feel sleeping in it every night?

"Well, if you're sure you don't mind. I bet the girls will have great fun sharing, won't you, girls?"

Sage and I look at each other. She gives me a hesitant smile, so I feel like I have to smile back.

"That's settled, then," Sage's mum says. "So, Emma, Allie, can you recommend some things for us to do in the village?"

"Well, there's a Knit and Natter group at the church on Thursdays," Mum says.

"Is there any yoga or Pilates?" Sage's mum asks.

I snort.

"There's Smile and Stretch on the village green on Saturday mornings," Mum tells her. "I suppose that's sort of like yoga."

Sage's mum looks skeptical, as she should. I've walked past the Smile and Stretch group loads of times, and they mostly seem to be exercising their jaws gossiping.

"How about for people your age, Allie?" Sage's mum asks. "What fun things are there for Sage to do in the village?"

I can't think of a single thing, but I don't want to say that. You'd think they would have done some research about the area before they agreed to do a house swap with us. I mean, they have Disneyland, Hollywood, the beach, and a pool. We have a walk through the village to buy a loaf of bread from Mrs. Armstrong, fields, sheep,

sheep, and more sheep. No wonder Sage's dad decided not to come. Sage told me he had to work in New York. The Big Apple—now that is a cool place to go on vacation. Why didn't they all just go there?

"You should introduce Sage to Chloe," Mum says to me.

"Chloe Belton? She's awful."

"Oh, Allie, she's not that bad. It would be nice for Sage to have someone to hang out with while she's here."

I give Sage a tiny shake of my head to show her that hanging out on her own would be way better than hanging out with Chloe Belton. Chloe will hate the fact that Sage is prettier than her. She doesn't like anyone being prettier than her, which is too bad because she always looks like she just swallowed a wasp.

"Why did you decide to come on holiday to Little Moleswood anyway?" I ask. "It's not exactly the place for an action-packed holiday. You could have gone to London. Or Paris. Or New York with your dad. Why didn't you do that?"

Sage stiffens and looks at her mum, who starts studying her nails.

"Allie!" Mum says, looking at me pointedly.

"What? I'm just saying. Who would choose Little Moleswood over New York? The best you could come up with was 'Knit and Natter,' 'Smile and Stretch,' and hanging out with Chloe Belton."

Sage's mum smiles, flashing her perfectly white teeth at me. I run my tongue over my braces and smile back without showing my teeth.

"Well, firstly," she says, "it's an incredibly beautiful place; secondly, we don't need action-packed, we want relaxing; and thirdly, we are on a mission, aren't we, Sage?"

"What kind of mission?" I ask, suddenly interested.

"Why don't you tell them, honey?"

"Well, we're researching our English relatives. My great-great-grandmother lived here. Her name was Violet," Sage says.

"Violet married Charles Wright, an American pilot who was stationed at an air base near here during the Second World War," Sage's mum says. "Sage is doing a school assignment all about our family tree, aren't you, honey?"

"Ah, that makes sense," Mum says. "We did wonder why you wanted to stay here. I mean, Little Moleswood is lovely and all, but, as Allie said, it's not the most exciting place in the world. You should ask Gwen Armstrong about your relatives. She owns the village shop and knows everyone and everything that goes on in Little Moleswood."

"Great. We'll do that after lunch. We're looking forward to exploring the village, aren't we, Sage."

That won't take them long. Dad always says that if you're driving through Little Moleswood and blink, you'll miss it.

"Now you mention the war, that reminds me, you should visit Bletchley Park. Allie loves it there. She makes us go every year for her birthday," Mum says, rolling her eyes.

"What's Bletchley Park?" Sage asks.

"It's amazing," I tell her. "It's a big old house near here. From the outside, it looks like, well, an ordinary big old house, but during the Second World War, it was the top secret headquarters for codebreakers."

"It is quite an interesting place," Mum says. "Well, it was the first couple of times we went."

I scowl at Mum. "Quite interesting! It's awesome. You can go inside the actual huts where they worked on cracking the codes and see the machines they used. It's amazing."

"I think I saw a movie about it," Sage's mum says.

I ignore her. "Anyway, experts say that the codes they cracked at Bletchley Park meant the war was four years shorter! Everything that happened there had to be kept top secret, or else the Germans would have bombed it.

The people who worked there couldn't tell anyone about what they did—not even their families."

"Wow," Sage says, looking impressed. Maybe she's not all sparkly silver nail polish and sunshine-blond hair. "Can we go, Mom?"

"Sure, honey. We'll add it to the list."

"I'm going to be a spy when I'm older," I announce.

Sage's mum looks at me in shock. I'm used to that—people often do look shocked when I tell them about my career plans, that or they laugh. It's annoying because when I'm older, and I am an actual spy, I won't be able to tell all those people who laughed at me what I do.

"Well, I wish I could show you around, but I should get some work done as we're still here," Mum says. "Mrs. Armstrong told the Drapers that our trip was delayed, and Maureen Draper called me to see if they could have an emergency appointment."

"What do you do, Emma?" Sage's mum asks.

"I'm a couples counselor. Half the village comes to see me."

Sage and her mum both look at her in surprise.

"And your neighbors are your clients? That must be awkward," Sage's mum says.

"Ha! The only awkward thing is that I charge for the advice. Everyone else in the village gives their opinion on their neighbors' relationships for free."

Sage's mum laughs hollowly, and it's Sage's turn to study her fingernails. Mum looks back and forth between the two of them.

"Oh," she says slowly as if she's solved a riddle. "Um, Allie, why don't you and I go and feed the chickens, and then you can help Sage get settled in your room."

"Why do we both need to feed the chickens?"

"Allegra," Mum says in "that" voice.

"Coming," I say.

CHAPTER TWELVE

SAGE
CURLS UP IN A BALL

"Ametrine powerfully combines amethyst and citrine and is a beautiful crystal that helps us see things in a new light. Do you need to take control of your life and move forward with a renewed sense of purpose? If so, ametrine could be the crystal for you." (from *Crystals A–Z*)

"I think I upset Allie when I laughed about their dog having gas. She's kind of prickly, isn't she?"

"Prickly" is a good word to describe Allie. If she were a porcupine, she'd shoot her quills at someone if they annoyed her. I'm more like a hedgehog who would curl up into a ball. I felt like curling up into a ball when Allie's mom told us that she's a couples counselor. I wonder if Mom and Dad did couples counseling. If they didn't, they should. You shouldn't be allowed to break up without trying your hardest to work things out, especially if you have kids, or in their case, *a* kid. Even Nora and Nico's parents saw a counselor. My parents should not use the same one. Maybe now that Mom knows Allie's mom is a counselor, she'll ask her for some advice. I think about Emma Greenwood's kind face and warm smile that makes her eyes crinkle—maybe she'd be able to help.

"You don't mind sharing a room with Allie for a couple of nights, do you?" Mom says, interrupting my thoughts. "I felt weird about being in Emma's room while she slept on a bunk bed."

I don't want to share a room with anyone. I want to be back home in my own room, but instead of saying I mind, I do what I seem to do all the time now—I say the easiest thing to say, the thing least likely to upset anyone. Anyone except me.

"I don't mind."

"Thanks, honey. Come on, let's go and explore the village. We can ask at the store if they know anything about Violet. I hope they've got some almond milk."

As we walk down the narrow street in the direction Mrs. Greenwood said would take us straight into the center of the village, Mom takes deep breaths, like she does when she's doing yoga.

"I'm so glad we came here. Aren't you? Everything seems so fresh and, I don't know, hopeful."

Mom is facing away from me, but I can hear the smile in her voice. She's taking pictures of the fields that stretch as far as you can see. They're dotted with hundreds of sheep—the ones farthest away look like cotton balls. English people really like sheep. Mom hasn't stopped taking pictures with her new camera since we arrived. She even took photos of Chickpea, Nestle, and Nugget but refused to go anywhere near Beeyoncé. She went pale when she found out there's a beehive in the garden. I wonder what she means about things seeming hopeful. Is she hopeful about her and Dad? Does she think that some time apart will help? People say that absence makes the heart grow fonder, but people also say "out of sight, out of mind," don't they?

"I'm going to send Grandma some pictures of the village," she says.

"You should send some to Dad too."

"I don't think Dad will be very interested in photos of the village. We'll send him some of you, though."

"I bet Dad would be interested. I bet he wishes he were here right now. With us."

"Hmmm," she says, fiddling with her camera. "I'm not sure I've got the shutter speed right for this light. I'll need to check the instructions when we get back to the cottage."

"Mom!"

"What?" she says, looking up from her camera.

"I said I bet Dad wishes he were here."

"I guess. Sage, look! That must be the church where your great-great-grandparents got married."

Mom points across the street to a small gray stone church, which is set back from the road. A blue sign with *St. Agatha's* written on it in swirly gold letters is hanging above the gate that leads into the churchyard and swaying gently in the breeze.

"We should have a look in the churchyard later," Mom says. "Maybe some of our Thornton ancestors are buried there. Let's go to the store first, though."

I don't really like the idea of looking at gravestones, so I happily follow Mom into the store. Maybe she'll forget about the idea.

A bell chimes cheerily as we open the door and walk inside, and a delicious smell of baking greets us. Now it's my turn to take deep yoga breaths. Allie told me that Mrs. Armstrong made that yummy cake we ate for breakfast. Maybe we can buy another one.

"Hello there," says a voice from the back of the store, and a small, rosy-cheeked lady appears carrying a plate of cookies. She has a cloud of tight white curls, a bit like the fleece of one of the sheep in the patchwork fields. She's wearing purple-framed glasses and a frilly white apron with purple flowers on it, and she has a smudge of flour on her cheek.

"You must be the American visitors staying at Cringle Cottage. Welcome to Little Moleswood. I'm Gwen Armstrong."

I wonder how she knows who we are. Mrs. Armstrong smiles at me as if she knows what I'm thinking.

"Emma told me you were arriving yesterday. There isn't much that happens in Little Moleswood that I don't know about. Lauren and Parsley, isn't it?" she says, beaming.

Parsley? Is she kidding me?

"Excuse me?" Mom says.

"Lauren and Parsley," Mrs. Armstrong repeats.

"It's Sage," Mom says. "I'm Lauren, and this is Sage."

"Oh, that's right. What a pretty name. I knew it was some type of herb. The lady who plays the organ at church is called Rosemary. I've never met a Sage before, though. I did think Parsley was an odd choice, but you never know these days."

As Mom and Mrs. Armstrong chat, I drift away from the counter to explore the small store. It reminds me of the Calico Critters Grocery Market I used to have— the one I secretly played with long after my friends had given their sets to a younger brother or sister. Life seemed so much easier in those days. My biggest worry back then was probably whether the Splashy Otters or the Tuxedo Cat family should be in charge of the grocery store. Just like in my Calico Critters store, all the items on the shelves have their labels neatly facing out, and the cans are stacked in tidy pyramids. The cereal boxes are even in alphabetical order: All-Bran, Cheerios, Coco Pops, Corn Flakes, etc. On one wall, there are sets of knitting needles sorted by size and dozens of balls of wool organized by color.

At the back of the shop is another counter, this one with a red-and-white sign above it saying *Post Office*. As I walk over to take a closer look, Mrs. Armstrong appears behind the counter like a genie from a lamp.

"Hello," she says. "Can I help you with anything, dear?"

"Um, no thank you."

"Maybe you could send your father a postcard. There's a lovely one of the village church."

How does she know that Dad isn't with us?

Mrs. Armstrong turns to Mom. "Emma told me your husband couldn't come on holiday with you because of his job. What a shame."

"Wow," Mom mutters. "How does anyone manage to keep anything private in this place?"

"Private?" Mrs. Armstrong throws her head back and laughs, sounding like the tinkling bell over the door. "Not in this village, dear."

"Let's get a postcard of the church to send to Grandma, and you pick one out for Dad," Mom says. "By the way,

Mrs. Armstrong, my great-grandparents got married at St. Agatha's Church. We're hoping to find out more about them."

"So that's why you're here. Emma did wonder why you'd want to swap your fancy house in California for a cottage in Little Moleswood. She says you have a swimming pool. Very posh! You Americans are keen on tracking down your relatives, aren't you? There was an American air base near here in the Second World War, so there are lots of people who can trace their family to the area, what with all those GI brides moving over there after the war."

"What's a GI bride?" I ask.

"It's what we call the English girls who married American soldiers and went to live in the United States. There were thousands of them across England. I can't remember what 'GI' stands for, though. It always makes me think of gastro intestinal, but that's just because of my stomach issues." Mrs. Armstrong laughs. "What was her name?"

"Violet. Violet Thornton before she got married," Mom says.

"Thornton," Mrs. Armstrong says, scrunching up her forehead deep in thought. "I can't think of any Thorntons living in Little Moleswood, but I've only been here ten years."

I look at Mrs. Armstrong in surprise. She seems like she's lived here forever—queen of Little Moleswood.

"You should check with the vicar. If your relatives got married at St. Agatha's, the records will be there. You'll have to come back tomorrow, though. I saw her drive off about an hour ago. She's probably gone to visit Malcolm. He's on his last legs. I'll probably need to get my black hat out before too long."

Mom and I look at each other in alarm.

"Oh, don't look so sad, dears. Malcolm's had a lovely long life—ninety-seven years old. Right, what else can I get for you?"

"The people here are super friendly, aren't they?" Mom says as we walk back to the cottage with our cake—this one is lemon drizzle flavor—some postcards and stamps, a loaf of bread, some strawberries and blackberries that Mrs. Armstrong told us she had picked in her garden yesterday evening, and a vegetable pie.

"It's a shame Mrs. Armstrong didn't have any almond milk at the store. You'd think there would be at least one lactose intolerant person in the village."

"It was weird she knew Dad didn't come with us, isn't it?"

"I guess that's life in an English village. I wouldn't like everyone knowing my business."

As we walk back past the church, I try to picture my great-great-grandparents standing smiling outside, surrounded by family and friends throwing confetti at them. In my mind, the people are all in black and white, like in the picture Grandma gave to me. I wonder if there were bridesmaids.

"Mom, did Violet have any brothers or sisters?"

"Not that Grandma found out about through her research, so I doubt it. An only child, just like you. The GI bride thing was interesting, wasn't it? Imagine having to leave your entire family to go live on the other side of the world, where you didn't know anyone."

"Except your husband," I say.

"Of course, but what if Violet wasn't happy? Maybe she wanted to come back to England. Maybe she missed her life here. People didn't get divorced much in those days."

"Or maybe she was happy and loved absolutely everything about her life in California—especially her husband."

"Maybe. I don't think I would have liked it, though. Violet was very young when she got married. She was only twenty-two."

"How old were you and Dad when you got married?"

"Twenty-seven."

"Well, twenty-seven isn't young at all."

"Let's see if you still think that when you're twenty-seven. Anyway, we're not talking about me, are we?"

Aren't we?

CHAPTER THIRTEEN

ALLIE
IS ON THE RUN

"Toby South looked really cute in The Wizard of Oz, *even though he was dressed as a scarecrow."* (from my diary)

When I go out to feed the chickens that afternoon, I pop my head into the Chick-Inn, hoping that my diary will have somehow magically reappeared since the last time I looked. Of course it hasn't. Max can't have hidden it in his bedroom, because I've searched it from top to bottom, so he must have taken it with him. Every time I think about Max having my diary, my blood boils so much that I'm surprised people can't hear it bubbling.

Chickpea clucks hello and studies me with her one open eye.

"You were supposed to be guarding it, Chickpea," I tell her as I close the chicken coop door behind me. "I hope you at least pecked him."

"Lost something?" says a nasal voice.

Ugh, Chloe Belton. I thought she was in Italy. She's been going on about it at school for weeks.

"No," I say.

"Who were you talking to?" she asks, looking around the garden.

"Nobody." It's not like I'm going to tell Chloe Belton that I was talking to a chicken.

Chloe raises an eyebrow in a "yeah right" way. "Aren't you supposed to be in California?"

I nod.

Chloe looks toward the house. "Is Max here?"

"No," I say, speaking slowly as if she was a little kid. "Maximilian is in California."

"So how come you're here?"

I give a long-suffering sigh. "It's a long story." And one that, quite frankly, is absolutely none of her business.

"Well, are you going to California or not?"

Wow, she's almost as relentless as Willow. I shrug. Luckily Chloe loses interest in me and turns to her favorite subject—herself.

"I just got back from Italy, which was amaaaaaaaaaz-ing. It was soooooo romantic! I met a gorgeous boy there called Luca, but don't tell Max."

Chloe Belton has a reaaaaaaaaaaaaally annoying way of speaking. Also, the fact that she is telling me this means that she absolutely wants me to tell Max, so I definitely won't. Max couldn't care less who Chloe likes. He's got a crush on Olivia Lee. I bet this boy Luca doesn't even exist.

"Amaaaaaaaazing," I say.

"Um, Allie?" Sage says, walking tentatively toward us.

It's weird that Sage isn't more confident, because if I looked like her and lived in a fancy house in California with a pool and my own bedroom, I would swan around like the queen, but American.

"Hi," Chloe Belton says in her fake-friendly voice. "You must be the American girl." She looks Sage up and down.

"No shizzle, Sherlock," I mutter.

Chloe scowls at me. "As Allie has zero manners, I'll introduce myself. I'm Chloe. I live here."

I roll my eyes. Talk about stating the obvious. If she didn't live there, why the heck would she be standing in the garden?

"Allie's probably told you all about me. I just got back from Italy. I'm in the same year as her brother at school. How old are you?"

"Eleven," Sage says.

"I'm thirteen," Chloe says. "But everyone says I look at least sixteen. I just got back from Italy. I met the cutest boy there. His name is Luca. It was sooooooo romantic."

Chloe pronounces "Luca" in what I think is supposed to be an Italian accent.

"Do you have any pictures of this Italian boyfriend?" I

ask, putting "Italian" and "boyfriend" in air quotes.

Chloe flushes. "They're on my phone, but it's charging."

I smirk. If Chloe Belton had photos of her with a cute Italian boy on her phone, she would be keeping it fully charged at all times. Either the Italian boy is a) not cute, or b) he doesn't exist. My money is on b.

"Well, we've got to go, haven't we, Sage?" I say, giving her a meaningful look. "We have to do that thing, you know, for our mums."

"Um, okay," Sage says hesitantly, and I take her hand and pull her in the direction of the cottage.

"Oh, Allie," Chloe says in a sly tone, "speaking of boyfriends, how is Toby?"

I stop dead in my tracks.

"What?" I ask in as casual a voice as I can manage, even though my heart is racing. I breathe out slowly, willing my burning cheeks to cool down before I turn around.

"Toby South. I heard you have a huuuuuuge crush on him."

"That's not true! I don't have a crush on him. Who told you that?"

"I couldn't possibly reveal my sources," Chloe says, smirking. "Anyway, don't you guys have to go and do that 'thing' for your mums?"

Chloe Belton smiles in her sickly-sweet way, flicks

her hair, and sashays back into her house. I stand, frozen to the spot, staring after her. She can't have heard that. It's not possible. I've never told anyone that I like Toby. Never. The only place I've ever admitted it is—oh no! Max wouldn't, would he?

"Allie? Are you okay?" Sage asks, looking at me with concern.

"My diary," I say in a shaky voice, a hideous fluttery feeling rising from my stomach to my chest. "My diary!"

A sob sticks in my throat and I do the only thing I can think of doing—I run. Over the back wall, across the fields, tears blinding me, I stumble and trip on clumps of grass, but I don't stop, and I don't look back. Not once.

CHAPTER FOURTEEN

SAGE
IS ON HER HEELS

"Blue chalcedony is known as the stone of friendship. It encourages laughter and good listening skills. Do you have a friend in need of your support? If so, blue chalcedony is the perfect crystal for you." (from Crystals A–Z)

Allie is fast, but I'm fast too. Fast enough to see her legs disappear as she scrambles under a giant prickly-looking bush. I bend over, winded from sprinting across two and a half fields, and hold my sides. I wonder if that awful girl Chloe watched Allie run away. The look on Chloe's face when she asked Allie about that boy was poisonous and pleased all at once. No wonder Allie can't stand her.

"Allie, are you okay?"

I wait, but there's no reply. I know that she can hear me, though, because I can hear her—she's breathing even harder than I am.

"I'm just going to sit right here," I say as if it's the most normal thing in the world to be talking to someone who is hiding in a bush, and sit down on the soft pillowy grass to wait. "We don't have to talk or anything."

I'd chased Allie across two fields of sheep, but I can't see any animals in this field, so I lie back and gaze at the blue chalcedony–colored sky. Soft, wispy clouds float lazily across it, and my arms and legs suddenly feel heavy. I let out a deep sigh. I wonder what time it is in LA. Maybe I'll close my eyes—just for a minute.

"I hate my brother!"

Allie's furious voice cuts through the quiet, and my eyelids snap open.

"What?" I ask, sitting up.

"He stole my diary."

"He did?"

"Yes. And what's even worse is that then he must have told Chloe Belton what I'd written, or maybe he even gave it to her to read."

Allie's voice trails off, and she sniffs loudly.

"Are you sure?" I ask tentatively. "That's really bad."

"How else would she know about me liking Toby? God, it's even worse than the time Max told her about the Pull-Ups. I'm going to flush his lucky swimming goggles down the toilet as soon as I get home."

Did she just say "pull-ups"? I have no idea what pull-ups have got to do with anything, and I really hope she doesn't try to flush swimming goggles down the toilet—they would definitely block it.

"Maybe Chloe doesn't know anything at all. Maybe she suspects you like that boy and was trying to get you to admit it. My friend Nora once did that to her brother. She told him she knew that he was the one who broke the remote control because she saw him do it on the Fur-Cam."

"The FurCam?" Allie says, suddenly sounding interested. "What's that?"

"It's to keep an eye on their dog, Pikachu. He used to get lonely when they weren't home and bark so much that the neighbors complained, so their mom got a camera so she can keep an eye on him while she's at work. She can talk to him if he barks. The FurCam can even give Pikachu a treat."

"Really?"

"Really."

"Did your friend see her brother break the remote?" Allie asks.

I'm glad that I've distracted her.

"Nope. The FurCam wasn't even turned on because they were all home. That's what I mean—Nora just pretending to Nico that she knew he'd done it made him admit it. Maybe that's what Chloe was doing."

"I don't think she's that smart," Allie says.

"You were right. She is awful!"

"Oh, she is, but my brother is way worse."

I think about this for a while.

"I've always wanted a brother or a sister."

"Ugh, no! You're so lucky to be an only child. My brother is a mean, smelly, loud, obnoxious show-off, and my sister is a little brat who follows me around all day and steals my stuff. My parents don't do anything to stop either of them. It's like I disappear because I'm in the middle. It's like I'm invisible."

I can't imagine anyone ever not seeing Allie. She's so bright and sparky you can see the energy coming off her—she crackles. Nobody could ignore her, even if they tried.

"It's like the way I always have to sit in the middle seat in the car," she says. "Max says his legs are too long, so he sits behind Mum. Mum and Dad say Willow's booster seat is safer behind Dad, so there I am, stuck in the middle. You could take up the whole back seat of your car if you wanted. I bet your parents even let you sit in the front."

I decide not to admit that Mom and Dad do sometimes let me sit in the front because I get carsick.

"Have you hidden here before?" I ask instead.

"Yes. Bear usually comes with me. One time I came here for the whole day, and nobody even noticed I was gone. I brought sandwiches and everything. When I told

Mum I could have been kidnapped, she just said, 'Well, I'm glad you weren't,' and Max said that the kidnappers would have paid my parents to take me back once they realized how annoying I am."

"Isn't it prickly in there?" I ask, touching one of the thorny branches lightly.

"It's okay once you get inside. It's getting in and out that's the problem."

I bet Mom's getting worried about me, but I don't want to say that to Allie after what she said about her family not noticing when she came here for the whole day.

"Maybe we should get back," I say.

No reply.

"I kind of need to pee."

"Just pee behind the wall," Allie says.

"I can't. What if someone sees me?"

"Someone like who? A sheep?"

"I don't know. A farmer or something."

Allie sighs, and, with a lot of ouches and muttering, she wriggles her way out of the bush. Her red hair is a mess, and she has small leaves and twigs poking out of it at random angles. She stands up and makes a half-hearted attempt to dust herself off.

"It's a good thing you're wearing jeans," I say, looking at her scratched arms. She looks as if she's been attacked by Pandora.

"Come on, then," Allie says. "Let's go. *Your* mum will probably be worried about *you*."

The sky is turning a violet-pink color by the time we reach the cottage. We didn't talk the whole way back. Allie seemed like she wanted to be quiet. She kept glancing at the house next door, probably checking to see if that awful girl Chloe was still in her garden.

Our moms are sitting at the small round wooden table on the terrace, where Allie and I ate our cake this morning—it feels like a really long time ago. Mom is resting her elbows on the table, her chin on her hands, and Mrs. Greenwood is patting her on the back as if she's comforting her. She must have been really worried. I hurry forward to tell Mom that I'm okay, but Allie grabs my arm and pulls me down into a crouch next to her.

"Ouch!" I say. "What did you do that for?"

"Shhhhhhhh! Let's listen. It looks like they're having an important conversation. I can tell by their body language. I'm an expert. Come on, let's get closer."

Allie crawls across the lawn army-style, and I follow her until we're close enough to hear.

"So that is why your husband didn't come with you. I did wonder," Mrs. Greenwood says.

Mom nods. "We just want to do what's best for Sage."

Allie pokes me hard in the ribs. I ignore her.

"Of course," Mrs. Greenwood says in a soothing voice, "there are no right or wrong answers. So, what's next?"

Mom says something in a really quiet voice. I wriggle forward, straining to hear her reply. Allie grabs me by the ankle, and I try to kick my leg free.

"Ouch!" says Allie.

"Allie?" Mrs. Greenwood says, peering in our direction. "Is that you?"

"Who else would it be?" Allie says, sounding cranky as she stands up.

"What on earth are you doing crawling around in the grass?"

"Sage dropped her ring."

"Hi," I say lamely, standing up next to Allie.

"There you are," says Mom. "I was worried about you."

"I told you they'd be absolutely fine," Mrs. Greenwood says. "Allie's always disappearing off somewhere."

"Nice to know *some* people's parents worry about them being kidnapped," Allie mutters.

Mrs. Greenwood laughs and ruffles her daughter's hair.

"Are you planning to let birds nest in there?" she asks, removing a couple of twigs and leaves. "You look like you've been dragged through a hedge backward."

"Are you okay, Mom?" I ask, walking over to her and taking her hand.

"I'm fine," she says, giving me a small smile and squeezing my hand. "I was just worried about you, that's all."

"Come on," Mrs. Greenwood says. "Let's go inside. Dinner isn't going to make itself. Allie, you can peel the potatoes."

Allie groans but follows her mom into the house.

"Would it be okay if I call Dad?" I ask Mom.

"Of course, honey."

"Do you want to speak to him?"

"I should help Emma with dinner. Tell Dad I said hi and that I'll speak to him soon."

I follow Mom inside, then trudge upstairs alone to call Dad. I don't know what Mrs. Greenwood is making for dinner, but my stomach feels like it does on long car rides, and I don't think I could swallow a single bite.

"Has anyone ever told you that you look like that girl from *Frozen*?" Allie asks, peering over the side of the top bunk.

I keep my eyes tightly closed and try to ignore her. I came to bed early so I could think—think about what Mom was going to tell Mrs. Greenwood and about my chat with Dad. He was outside when I called him, and I could hear the New York soundtrack of cars honking and people yelling in the background. I tried to sound happy when I talked to him. I told him all about Allie and Mrs. Greenwood still being at Cringle Cottage when we arrived and Bear being sick. I didn't tell him that I'd heard Mom and Mrs. Greenwood talking.

"That must have been awkward," he said. "I'll bet your mom wasn't happy."

"She wasn't. And she can't find any almond milk here. The lady in the village store said she should try mixing some almonds with regular milk!"

Dad laughed. "I'd love to have seen your mom's face when she said that."

"I miss you, Dad. We both do."

"I miss you too, honey. I'll give you a call in the morning. Sleep tight."

"Sage! I know you're only pretending to be asleep," Allie says, interrupting my thoughts. "It's so obvious. I can tell by your breathing. It's too shallow. So, have they?"

"No," I say with a sigh, opening my eyes. "Can you turn the light out? I just want to go to sleep."

"I'm really surprised nobody ever told you that. Willow is obsessed with Elsa. She'd probably dress you up in an ice-blue snowflake princess dress if she were here. We should take a photo of you next to the Elsa pillow and send it to her."

I don't reply. I just want the light out and to be on my

own, or as on my own as I can be, with Allie lying above me.

"It's weird sharing a room with you," she says. "You're so quiet! I'm used to Willow, who literally doesn't stop talking until she falls asleep. She crashes out mid-sentence, mid-word even. Luckily, I have earplugs."

I wonder if she has a spare pair.

"You're so lucky to have your own room. I wish I did," she says.

Allie sighs when I don't answer, and the mattress creaks as she turns over and snaps out the light.

"Fine. Night, then," she says, sighing again.

"Good night."

After a few seconds, Allie turns the light back on, and her head reappears over the side of the bunk.

"What do you think your mum was going to say to my mum?"

"What do you mean?"

"Before you made all that noise and blew our cover earlier. You'd make a terrible spy, by the way. What do you think they were talking about?"

"I don't know."

Allie studies me. "I think you do."

"I don't."

"I've trained myself to read facial expressions, and I think you do. Why didn't your dad come on holiday?"

"Because he had to wo—"

"—and don't say because he had to work, because we both know that's not true. Are your parents splitting up?"

My breath catches in my throat. It's the first time anyone has said it out loud.

"I don't know," I say quietly.

"Why don't you just ask your mum?"

"I don't want to."

"Why not?"

"I don't know how to."

Allie gives me a "how hard can it be?" look. "You just say, 'Mum,' or in your case, 'Mom, are you and Dad getting a divorce?' Easy."

"Would you ask your parents?"

"I wouldn't need to. I'd probably know before they did. It's one of the reasons I'll be a great spy. I can read the room."

I don't tell Allie that I'm worried that even saying the words aloud might make it real. That asking the question might set off a reaction, like a butterfly flapping its wings in the Amazon causing a storm in LA. My science teacher talked about that once. It's called chaos theory. She said that tiny changes in atmospheric pressure could lead to major changes in the path of a storm. Maybe the butterfly flapped its wings months or even years ago.

Allie turns off the light again and flicks it right back on.

"Would you like me to ask your mum for you? I'll do it in a supersubtle way. In *Think Like a Spy*—you can borrow it if you like—there's a whole chapter on covert interrogation techniques. Basically, you just slip an important question into a casual conversation."

"No! Please don't say anything to my mom."

"It's a shame the lie detector test I ordered online hasn't arrived yet. We could have tried it out on your mum. The real ones cost hundreds of pounds, but this is a toy one. It gives mild electric shocks if you lie. It has over two thousand five-star reviews!"

"Allie, please don't say anything."

"Are you sure?"

"I'm sure."

Allie sighs. "Your loss."

"Promise?"

"Promise."

I don't know if I believe her, but Allie snaps off the light and doesn't turn it back on again. After a few minutes, I hear her snoring quietly. I thought she might not be able to sleep either—that maybe she'd lie awake worrying about her missing diary and figuring out how to get it back from her brother. I wish the biggest thing I had to worry about was some stupid diary and people finding out I liked a boy. It's not as if people knowing you have a crush on someone will change your entire life, but finding out for sure what is going on with my parents could literally crack my life and my heart into two. What's going to happen to me? I don't want to live in two houses, sleep in two beds, keep my clothes in two dressers, and have my heart in two different places, maybe two miles apart like the twins, maybe even farther. At least Nora and Nico have each other. A wave of loneliness washes over me. I hate being the only person who knows exactly what is going on inside my head. It's scary. I feel tears well up and try and fail to stop them before they slide down my cheeks onto Elsa's.

CHAPTER FIFTEEN

ALLIE
IS BACK AT THE VET'S OFFICE

"I calculated that last week I spent approximately 89% of my waking hours doing things I didn't want to do." (from my diary)

There's no lonelier sound in the world than the noise someone makes trying to cry silently. Sage did her best last night, but I have excellent hearing. I wanted to make her feel better, but I definitely didn't. She was so nice to me yesterday, just sitting and waiting for me to talk instead of telling me what I should do. Maybe I should be a bit more like that. I didn't think I'd like Sage when I first met her, what with her perfect silver nails and golden hair, but she reminds me of the cupboard under the stairs, all neat-looking from the outside, but when you open the door, junk spills out everywhere. I wonder if it's better to look like a mess on the outside if you're one on the inside. It's too bad she won't just ask her mum what's going on, or better yet, have me do it for her. It's good to know things, even the bad things, especially the bad things. Like now I know that my brother showed Chloe Belton my diary, but what I don't know is what I'm going to do about it. What's that saying about revenge being a dish best served cold? Well, my brother and Chloe Belton are going to be eating frozen dog food if I get my way. Without my diary, my feelings have nowhere to go. Maybe that's why I told Sage yesterday about feeling invisible. I've never said that out loud before. I'm going to help her, whether she wants me to or not.

Bear is wide awake when Mum and I go to pick him up. His eyes are shining, his tail is wagging, and when I kiss him on the top of his lovely head, he even smells like his old self. In fact, apart from the enormous white plastic cone around his neck, which he has to wear to stop him from licking his stitches and the dressing on his tummy, he looks as good as new. Well, he does look a bit sillier than usual wearing that collar—like a cross between Queen Elizabeth the First in her white frilly neck ruffle and a scoop of chocolate ice cream in a cone. His cone doesn't stop him from being able to lick my face. I've got a feeling Sage and her mum won't like having their faces licked. It's easier just to give in to Bear's face licks, though. If you try to wriggle away, it just makes him more determined to give you a thorough wash.

When we get back to Cringle Cottage, I follow Bear

into the kitchen. Sage's mum's eyes get even wider and rounder than usual when she sees him, and she actually takes a step back.

"Wow! He's enormous! I mean, I know you said that he's a big dog, but he's . . ."

"The size of a small pony," Mum says, looking at Bear fondly.

"What kind of dog is he?" Sage asks, cautiously patting Bear's side. You can tell she's not used to being around dogs—especially not dogs as big as Bear, but at least she's trying.

"He's a Newfoundland. He's super friendly," I tell her. "Isn't he the best dog you ever saw?"

"He's the biggest dog I ever saw. Is he always like this?" Sage's mum asks, watching Bear as he joyfully runs laps of the table, bumping into chairs as he goes.

I read somewhere that cats can measure distances with their whiskers, so they know which gaps they can fit through. That is clearly not the case for dogs and neck cones—well, for this dog at least.

"He is a bit subdued," Mum says. "Don't worry, though. I'm sure he'll be back to his usual bouncy self in no time."

Sage and her mum exchange nervous glances.

"What do you have planned for the rest of the day?" Mum asks, probably trying to distract Sage's mum from the fact that she has agreed to take care of a cone-wearing, horse-size dog for the rest of her vacation.

"We're going to go talk to the vicar and see if we can find out more about Violet."

"That sounds fun," Mum says, "doesn't it, Allie?"

Actually, it sounds totally boring, but it would be really rude to say that, so I just "mm-hmm" in reply and try to keep Bear still long enough to put his collar back into place. He pants and smiles at me. Max says dogs can't smile, but Bear can.

"Allie will go with you," Mum says. "Won't you, Allie?"

I give Mum a "way to throw me under the bus" look and then turn to Sage's mum, trying my best to smile sweetly.

"I'd love to, but I need to stay here and look after Bear," I say in a disappointed voice.

"No, you don't," Mum says. "Bear needs to rest, and he's not going to settle down with you here. You go with Lauren and Sage, and Bear can stay here with me while I make sure everything is ready for tomorrow. I can't believe we're finally going to sunny California." Mum looks out of the window at the drizzle. "Best not wait for it to stop raining before you head out—it might be a while. Umbrellas are in the cupboard under the stairs. Be careful when you open the door."

✴ ✶ ✴

On the way to the church, Sage's mum stops to take photographs every two minutes, even though it's raining. Everything she sees is "adorable," "super cute," or "quaint," and she seems to be having a great time. In fact, she looks the happiest I've ever seen her, even though it's raining and it sounds like she's probably getting a divorce. Sage's mum is going to have hundreds of sheep photos by the end of the trip. Americans seem to really like sheep. Do they not have them in California? Sage's mum makes her stand next to the postbox to take a photo of her posting cards. Apparently, our ordinary postbox is "just wonderful" because it's red. I have no idea what color Californian postboxes are. Even if they're fluorescent pink with purple spots, I can't imagine caring enough to take a picture of one.

Sage looks about as unhappy as her mum looks cheerful. Even her hair looks depressed. She has dark circles under her eyes, which are red from last night's silent sob-athon. I'm surprised her mum hasn't noticed. I guess she's too busy taking photos of postboxes and sheep. Maybe she has more in common with my parents than I thought. I scowl at her back. Parents should pay attention.

"Pssst!" I say, tugging Sage's arm while her mum starts taking photos of the telephone box. "I had an idea last night while I was asleep. I often have my best ideas when I'm sleeping. Sometimes I can't remember them in the morning, but luckily, I did today. Step one is to get your mum's phone. She's always texting. If we can see who she's texting, maybe we can figure out what she's up to."

"What do you mean, what she's up to?"

"Well, I hate to say it, but she probably has a boy-friend. I did a search this morning and, according to Google, around twenty percent of divorces in America are due to cheating."

Sage looks as if I've slapped her.

"My mom isn't cheating!"

"I guess it could be your dad. Anyway, the only way to find out is to get her phone. It's not like we can check your dad's. I'll do it; I'm good at this kind of thing. She'll never even know we took it."

"You're not taking my mom's phone, Allie. This is none of your business. You don't even know us."

"Well, actually, it kind of is my business because you're staying at my house and you need my help. It's fate. I mean, if Bear hadn't got sick, you and I would never have met, and you'd be stuck here in Little Moleswood not knowing what to do."

I hurry Sage and her mum straight to the back of the church before her mum can stop to take a gazillion photos of the stained glass windows—although they would make a nice change from all the sheep—and lead them through to the community room. It's the place where Knit and Natter, Smile and Stretch (if it's raining), Heavenly Flowers, Tots and Tambourines, and Holy Guacamole (the vicar's Taco Tuesday evening) happen. The Heavenly Flowers club must have had their meeting this morning, because Reverend Stella is sweeping up pink and red petals, twigs, and leaves from underneath the table.

Some people in Little Moleswood were upset when the new vicar arrived. Those same people still call her the new vicar even though she's been here for five years. They were upset because **ONE**, Reverend Stella is a woman, and **TWO**, she has blue streaks in her hair, which, combined with **THREE**, her bizarre fashion choices—today she's wearing a T-shirt that says *Jesus Follower, Taco Lover, Nap Taker* on it—plus the fact that **FOUR**, she sometimes roller-skates in church all add up to **FIVE**, her being a very un-vicar-like vicar. She's also about one hundred years younger than the last vicar. I like her a lot.

"Hi, Allie. How's Bear doing? You must be Lauren and Sage," Reverend Stella says, stretching out her hand, which Sage's mum goes to shake and ends up getting a fist bump. "Welcome to St. Agatha's. How about a cup of tea? Mrs. Armstrong told me that you're lactose intolerant. I only have regular milk. Sorry about that."

"Wow, everyone really does know everything in this village, don't they?" Sage's mum says.

Reverend Stella grins. "Equally cursed and blessed. There's the most wonderful sense of community here in Little Moleswood, but it's terrible if you prefer not to know about the farmer's hemorrhoids."

Sage's mum shudders.

"Allie, why don't you put the kettle on. I've got some of Mrs. Armstrong's chocolate chip shortbread, and there should be some homemade lemonade left over from the Heavenly Flowers ladies. Now, Sage, I hear you're trying to track down some relatives of yours."

I head over to the small kitchen area to get the tea, shortbread, and lemonade and listen while Sage and her mum tell Reverend Stella about great-great-whoever-it-is they are trying to find out about. As nobody is taking any notice of me, I grab a piece of shortbread, the crumbly, buttery, sugary yumminess melting on my tongue, then carry the tray over to the table and set it down.

"I did a bit of digging after Mrs. Armstrong told me your great-great-grandmother's name, and I found something that might interest you," Reverend Stella says.

She picks up a large dark green leather-bound book

and flicks through it before pushing it across the table toward Sage and her mum.

"These are the parish records for 1945 and 1946. I thought that if Violet married a pilot from the US Air Force base, they probably got married right after the war ended. Sure enough, here they are."

CERTIFIED COPY OF AN ENTRY OF MARRIAGE						
Pursuant to the Marriage Acts, 1811 to 1939						
Registration District: Moleswood						
Marriage Solemnized at						
The Parish Church of St. Agatha, Little Moleswood						
When Married	Name and Surname	Age	Condition	Rank or Profession	Residence at the Time of Marriage	Father's Name and Surname
14th February, 1946	Charles William Wright Jr.	26	Bachelor	Lieutenant United States Army Air Forces	RAF Fairford, Gloucestershire	Charles Wright Sr.
	Violet Elizabeth Thornton	22	Spinster	Nurse	Moleswood House, Little Moleswood, Gloucestershire	Thomas Thornton

"Wow, thank you! This is amazing," says Sage's mum. "Can we make a photocopy?"

"I already made one for you," Reverend Stella says, handing Sage's mum a piece of paper. "By the way, Moleswood House is just on the outskirts of the village. Allie, maybe you could take Lauren and Sage to see it? It's been empty for as long as I can remember, but a family from Oxford is moving in soon. Derek Armstrong is working up there today. I'm sure he won't mind you having a look around. Gwen told me that Derek told her that the tiles he's putting in the bathroom came all the way from Italy. They must have cost a fortune. I wonder if the new people will donate to the church roof fund?"

"It would be so special to see where Violet lived," Sage's mum says. "If you don't mind taking us, Allie."

"It's still raining," I say, trying to look disappointed. "We'll get soaked."

"Well, Lauren, Sage, if you'll excuse me, I must go and change before the bishop arrives. God wouldn't mind the T-shirt, but the bishop is a bit of a fuddy-duddy. Oh, I almost forgot, I found something else. Here you go. Let me know how you get on with your research, won't you?"

Reverend Stella hands Sage's mum two more pieces of paper and hurries out of the room.

"It's a record of Violet's baptism in 1924 and—oh, wow, a baptism record for Lily Thornton," she says. "Look, she was baptized in 1920. Lily must be Violet's older sister."

"Cool," I say. Now we can go home.

Sage's mum glances out of the window.

"Oh, look! It's stopped raining. We can go and see Moleswood House. Do you mind taking us, Allie?"

Ugh, I think.

"Okay," I say.

CHAPTER SIXTEEN

SAGE
IS UNCOVERING THE PAST

"Fluorite is one of the best crystals for mental focus. Do you have an important test or project coming up? If yes, fluorite may be the perfect stone for you." (from *Crystals A–Z*)

"**H**ello, where are you three going in such a hurry?" Mrs. Armstrong says, poking her head out of the store.

"Moleswood House," Allie says in a sulky voice. "It's where Sage's great-great-whoever lived."

"Ooh, my Derek is working up there today. The whole place is being redone for the new people," Mrs. Armstrong says. "You'll never believe it; they had tiles shipped all the way from—"

"Italy," Allie says. "Reverend Stella told us."

"Exactly! Must have cost a fortune. Anyway, I can't stand here chatting with you lot all day. By the way, Lauren, I managed to get some of that almond milk you've been on about. Why don't you pop in later and pick it up? Nobody else is going to buy it."

Moleswood House is about a ten-minute walk from the village store. It is made from the same sandy-colored stone as Cringle Cottage but about twice as big. Parked in front of the house is a blue van with *Derek Armstrong and Sons* written on the side in white letters. A gray-haired man with a bushy beard is sitting on a deck chair next to the van reading a newspaper.

"Hi, Mr. Armstrong," says Allie.

"Hello there, Allie. Don't you tell Gwen you caught me slacking off, will you?"

"I would never," she says, grinning at him.

"And how's that dog of yours doing?"

"Much better. Dr. Ted's amazing."

Mr. Armstrong turns and grins at Mom and me.

"And you must be the American visitors my wife keeps talking about. She said you can't drink real milk," he says to Mom. "Sorry to hear that."

Mom just smiles politely. She seems to be getting used to everyone in the village knowing everything about us.

"We wondered if it would be okay for us to have a look around the house," Mom says. "We've just come from the church, and apparently, our relatives used to live here."

"Fine by me," Mr. Armstrong says. "Make sure you check out the tiles in the bathroom."

"The ones from Italy," Allie says.

"Must have cost a fortune," Mom says.

Mr. Armstrong nods. "That's exactly what my Gwen said."

Inside, the house smells of fresh paint, all of it white. Dad would approve. We wander from empty room to empty room, our footsteps echoing on the polished wooden floorboards.

"We should probably have taken our shoes off," Mom whispers as Allie clatters ahead of us, leading the way to the back of the house.

The inside of Moleswood House doesn't match the outside, and nothing about it makes it feel like the place where my great-great-grandmother grew up. Maybe I was expecting dusty old rooms decorated with faded floral wallpaper and heavy velvet curtains. I wanted it to look as if my relatives had just left. Instead, Moleswood House looks as if they were never here.

The kitchen looks out over endless fields, just like the view from the kitchen window at Cringle Cottage. That's about the only thing the two rooms have in common, though. This kitchen reminds me of the one at home—all shiny polished silver appliances and white tiles—it's nothing like the kitchen at Allie's house, with its brightly painted walls, crowded mismatched furniture, and constant buzz of activity.

"There you are," says Mr. Armstrong, coming into the kitchen. "I suppose I should give this to you."

He hands Mom a small brown suitcase with a tiny gold padlock. The leather is worn and cracked.

"I found it in the attic yesterday when we were patching up the roof. I'm not sure who else to give it to. This place has been empty for as long as we've lived here."

Mom frowns as she studies the bag. "I mean, I don't know if we should take it. It could have nothing to do with our family."

"But the house did belong to your relatives," Mr. Armstrong says. "You may as well take it."

"Cool, let's open it!" Allie says, reaching for the bag.

"Thank you, Mr. Armstrong," Mom says, moving it out of Allie's reach. "I'll let Gwen know what's in here. If it doesn't seem to have belonged to anyone in our family, I'll give it to her. She'll know what to do with it."

"She seems to know what to do with everything," Mr. Armstrong says, chuckling. "Over the years, I've decided it's best to agree with her. What's that they say? Happy wife, happy life."

Back at Cringle Cottage, Allie taps her foot, rolls her eyes, and sighs a lot while Mom explains to Mrs. Greenwood what happened at the church and at Moleswood House.

"Now can we open it?" Allie says. "I'll do it."

"Um, Allie," Mrs. Greenwood says, "it's not your bag. I'm sure Lauren or Sage would like to open it themselves."

Mom hands me the bag with a smile. "Why don't you open it, honey?"

The leather is soft and warm as if it had soaked in a hundred years of sunshine. I wonder who the last person to hold it was—well, except for Mr. Armstrong, Mom, and now me. Maybe it was my great-great-grandmother.

"Come on, Sage," Allie says, hopping from foot to foot while I struggle with the little gold padlock. Who knows where its tiny gold key might be?

"Let me try," Allie says. "I taught myself to pick locks ages ago."

"Maybe Sage doesn't want you to pick the lock," Mrs. Greenwood says.

"I bet I can open it in less than a minute."

"Really?" I ask.

"She probably can," Mrs. Greenwood says. "She's always picking the lock to the bathroom when Willow locks herself in there."

"I just need a paper clip," Allie says. "There'll be one in the 'everything' drawer."

Mom and I look at her.

"We call it the 'everything' drawer because there's

everything you could ever need in there," her mom explains, "and it sounds way better than the 'stuff we can't be bothered to find a proper home for' drawer."

After quite a bit of rummaging around in the drawer, Allie finds a paper clip. She unbends one of the loops until the wire is straight and then wiggles it around in the lock, biting her lip with concentration and listening carefully. She looks like a thief opening a bank vault in a movie.

"Got it," she says triumphantly, taking off the padlock and clicking open the case.

"Allie," Mrs. Greenwood says in a warning voice, nodding in my direction.

"Fine," Allie says with a big sigh and slides the case across the table to me.

I open it slowly, and a soft smell of flowers and secrets wafts out. It almost feels as if the suitcase is sighing.

"Sage, stop!" Allie yells, making everyone jump. "You should wear gloves before you touch anything."

"It's not a crime scene," Mrs. Greenwood says.

"It could be. Sage's relatives could have been jewelry thieves for all we know."

Ignoring Allie, I open the suitcase wide, resting the lid gently against the table. It is lined with the palest green fabric that has tiny white flowers embroidered on it. Inside the bag are some brown folders, a dark green box about the size of a shoebox, two large books with faded navy-and-gold leather covers, some cream-colored lace fabric, and a small bunch of dried white flowers tied with a purple ribbon.

"What are the books?" Allie asks.

I pick one up to examine the front.

"Dictionaries. Oxford English Dictionaries."

"Dictionaries? Why the heck would anyone keep dictionaries locked away in a suitcase?" she says.

I shrug and open the *A–L* dictionary to the first page, and there, in faded brown ink, is the name of its owner. Lily Grace Thornton. I trace the words with my finger and turn the book around to show Mom.

"Wow!" she says, grinning. "That is so cool. You're actually holding your great-great-great-aunt's book."

Allie, who doesn't look as if she thinks it's particularly cool at all, leans over my shoulder.

"What's in the box?"

I lift the lid carefully. Inside are dozens of black-and-white photographs. The picture on the top of the pile shows two little girls wearing white dresses with big white bows in their hair, holding hands in front of Moleswood House.

"Do you think that's Violet and Lily?" I ask Mom.

"It must be."

Mrs. Greenwood leans over to look at the photograph.

"How wonderful. It's a case full of family memories."

"A case full of gold and diamonds would have been way cooler," Allie mutters.

Mom, Mrs. Greenwood, and I sit at the kitchen table for ages looking through the photographs and papers while Allie sprawls out in the striped armchair in the corner, her legs hanging over one arm, engrossed in her spy book.

"And the suitcase is really ours to take home?" I ask Mom.

"I guess so. We're Lily's only surviving relatives. I can't wait to show Grandma. I never thought we'd find something like this. It's just amazing."

"Let's call Dad and tell him."

"You call. I need to go to the store to collect the almond milk Mrs. Armstrong got for me."

"I'll wait until you get back."

"No, you go ahead. I can speak to him later."

I sigh. Would it really be such a big deal for her to call Dad before she goes to get the milk? Just another excuse. I think about asking her why she can't just pick it up after we've called him but decide not to bother. It's not like she's going to tell me.

"Can I use your phone? Mine's almost out of battery."

Mom passes me her phone.

"I'll come with you, Lauren," says Mrs. Greenwood. "I

need to pick up a few things. Bye, girls."

As soon as our moms leave the room, Allie drops her book and leaps out of the armchair.

"Genius!" she says.

"What?"

"Genius way to get your mum's phone. Now we can check her texts and emails to see if she's talking to a divorce lawyer or . . . a boyfriend!"

I scowl at her. "I didn't take it so we could do that. I really am borrowing it to call my dad. My phone is about to die."

Allie looks disappointed in me.

"Well, now you have it, it seems a shame not to take a quick look."

"No! We can't."

"Sure we can. Do you know her password?"

"Allie, I'm not going to look at my mom's texts."

"Here, pass me the phone. I'll do it. Do you want to know what's going on, or don't you?"

Do I? I'm not sure, but I hand her the phone doubtfully.

"Password?" she asks.

"One-two-three-four-five-six."

Allie looks up in horror. "Are you kidding? That is literally the most stupid password in the entire world."

She shakes her head, types in the password, and starts scrolling through the texts.

"Wow, your mum texts a lot. Who's Kristen?"

"My mom's best friend. Allie, give me the phone. You shouldn't be looking at my mom's messages."

"Well, then you won't want to hear that Kristen has given your mum the number of her divorce lawyer, will you?"

I grab the phone out of Allie's hands and start to read.

CHAPTER SEVENTEEN

ALLIE
HAS A PLAN

"It's so weird that the Secret Intelligence Service has a careers section on their website. Shouldn't that be a secret?" (from my diary)

So much for Sage not wanting to read the messages—now she's started, she can't stop. She's been scrolling through them for fifteen minutes while I keep watch at the window for our mums. I suggest we take pictures of some of the most incriminating evidence—mostly in the endless text chain between Sage's mum and Kristen. We have the shock of our lives when Kristen texts us, I mean she texts Sage's mum, while we're reading the messages.

I hear the reliable squeak of the garden gate. More people should let their gates' hinges get creaky. It's a good early warning system.

"Quick. They're coming. Your mum has the almond milk."

Sage looks up at me with a broken expression on her face. After the text messages we've just read, she probably doesn't care about the almond milk.

"Why don't you go and call your dad now?" I say.

Maybe it will make her feel better, and it will help with the cover story. It's always best to stay as close to the truth as possible.

Sage shakes her head.

"Well, your mum is going to know something's wrong as soon as she sees your face. You look as if you've seen a ghost. Let's go out into the garden before she comes in. I know Chloe Belton isn't there because I saw her leaving with her dad earlier. We can pretend we're cleaning out the Chick-Inn. Actually, I really do need to clean it out. You can help. Also, we should block Kristen on your mom's phone. She seems like a bad influence."

"We can't block Kristen. She's my mom's best friend."

"Fine, but let's go, quick."

"So," I say when we arrive at the Chick-Inn. "What do we know from our surveillance operation?"

"That my parents are getting a divorce," Sage says quietly.

Chickpea, who is very empathetic, clucks at her kindly. Nestle and Nugget ignore Sage and carry on scratching the ground. They're right for a change: this is no time for empathy and wallowing in misery—it's a time for action.

"You sweep, I'll shovel," I say, handing Sage an old

broom. "I'll summarize. We know that **ONE**, your mum's friend has given her the number of a divorce lawyer called Stephanie Salinas, who **TWO**, charges a ridiculous seven hundred and fifty dollars per hour, which **THREE**, seems very expensive without even counting the fact that **FOUR**, Stephanie Salinas also wants a five-thousand-dollar retainer, whatever that is, but **FIVE**, your mum hasn't paid her any money yet, so **SIX**, she might still be making up her mind about getting a divorce, which is why **SEVEN**, we need a plan, stat."

"A plan to do what?"

"A plan to do something. Anything! It doesn't seem like your mum has got a boyfriend, yet, and she does seem sad about the divorce, so maybe it's not too late. My mum says most of her clients' relationships could probably be fixed if they spent a week locked in the same room without distractions."

"You think we should lock my parents in a room together?"

"Maybe, but first, we need to get them into the same room."

"How are we supposed to do that when they're not even in the same country?"

"That's the bit I still need to figure out."

Sage looks at me, worry written all over her face.

"I'll think of something," I tell her.

"Girls, time to come in for dinner," Mum calls from the back door. "Make sure you give your hands a good wash. Don't forget that chicken poop can give you salmonella."

Sage trails after me. Salmonella seems to be the least of her worries.

Over dinner, I manage to tune out Mum's conversation with Sage's mum about things to do in California. I've trained myself to let other people's conversations wash over me so I can think about more interesting things. It's like being able to switch on an internal white noise machine, and by the time I've finished my enormous serving of apple crumble with custard, I have a plan.

"Okay, hear me out," I tell Sage when we're safely up in my room. "This might sound crazy, but you know that movie *The Parent Trap*, where the twins swap places to get their parents back together?"

Sage looks at me like I've got two heads. "What?"

"The movie. *The Parent Trap*. Have you seen it?"

"Yes. My best friends are twins. We used to watch it all the time."

"Well, I think we need to do something like that to

get your parents face-to-face."

"Um, I don't have a twin," she says.

"Obviously, I know that! You don't need a twin. The first step in the plan is to get your parents in the same country. In the movie, one parent is in America and the other one's in England, so they get their mum to America."

"You mean we'd get my mom to go to New York?" Sage asks, looking confused.

"No, we should get your dad to come here."

"But how would we do that?"

"You'll pretend you're sick, and he'll fly here. Easy."

"What would be wrong with me?"

Wow. Sage does not have a great imagination. Apparently, I'm going to have to do all the work.

"Appendicitis. I had my appendix taken out last year, so I can tell you exactly what symptoms you need to fake."

Sage shakes her head. "That won't work. I had my appendix taken out in February."

"Fine. Tonsillitis."

"I had them taken out last year."

"Jeez, have you had anything else taken out?"

"Adenoids," she says, folding and unfolding the hem of her dress. "I guess I could run away."

"Run away?"

"Yeah. If I ran away, Mom would be crazily worried, and Dad would come over to help find me."

I consider this for a minute but can imagine Sage's parents scouring the nearby fields for her, maybe using Bear as a sniffer dog. I don't think Bear would make a good sniffer dog, but maybe I should give it a try. I don't know why I didn't think of it before.

"No. We need something that won't make your parents call the police, which is the first thing they'd do if you went missing. Look how worried your mum was when we went to sit in a field for an hour. The police would search for you in a helicopter with one of those huge spotlights like they do in movies, and then we'd be in loads of trouble. Well, you would be. I'll be in California."

"How about I pretend my mom is sick? I could call Dad and tell him that Mom is in the hospital, and I'm home alone," says Sage.

I look at her, impressed. "That is actually an awesome idea."

"The only problem is he'd call Mom."

"Easy. You hide her cell phone. Then your dad won't be able to reach her."

"Do you think this will work, Allie?"

"One hundred percent," I say. "Definitely."

I actually don't think the plan will work at all, but even the idea of having a plan seems to be cheering Sage up. It's not like she's going to do it anyway.

"We've got this," I say, giving her an encouraging smile.

CHAPTER EIGHTEEN

SAGE
IS NOT CONFIDENT

"The golden topaz promotes deep friendships and reminds you to value true friends. It's a fun, sunny crystal that brings a real sense of joy. Are you looking for a special gem for a true friend? If so, the golden topaz might be the crystal for you." (from *Crystals A–Z*)

'm not sure why Allie keeps saying, "We've got this." She's leaving for California in exactly eight hours, so she doesn't have to get anything. I do—on my own.

"If you think about it," Allie says, "what we have to do is way easier than what they had to do in *The Parent Trap*. The girls in the movie had to learn to speak in completely different accents. Plus, they had to change their hair, one of them had to pierce her ears, and they had to trick their families into believing that they were someone else. It was only that dog in America that knew it was the wrong twin. So, here's the plan. I've written down every single step for you. All you need to do is, well, do it."

Allie hands me a sheet of paper.

TOP SECRET MISSION
PARENT TRAP

PHASE ONE:
GET YOUR DAD TO ENGLAND

1. *Steal your mum's phone and hide it—don't forget to turn off the ringer.*
2. *Deny having seen the phone. (If your mum uses advanced interrogation techniques—covered in chapter six of* Think Like a Spy—*then say you need to go to the loo.)*
3. *Go somewhere your mum can't overhear you, call your dad, and convince him that your mum is sick.*
4. *Tell him she is in hospital and can't talk right now. (I did think maybe you could say she was in a coma, but he might think she's dying, and if he does still love her, he'll be upset. She needs to be sick but not too sick.)*
5. *If your dad asks for the number of the hospital, give him a fake number.*
6. *Tell him you will stay with Mrs. Armstrong until he arrives.*

7. *He'll ask to speak to Mrs. Armstrong. Tell him*
    she'll call him back.
8. *Call me, and then I'll call him and pretend to*
    be Mrs. Armstrong.

"So, have you decided what you're going to say is wrong with your mum?"

"I'm going to tell him she got stung by a bee. Mom's allergic to bee stings. She can have a pretty bad reaction if she doesn't have her EpiPen. I can pretend she left it in California."

Allie looks impressed.

"Wow, no wonder she didn't want to come and meet Beeyoncé. I love this idea. All the best cover stories have factual elements."

"What if my dad says he won't come?"

Allie rolls her eyes again.

"Is your dad nice?"

"Very."

"Then, when he gets a call from his daughter who tells him that she is all alone in a strange country while her mum is in hospital with a potentially deadly reaction to a bee sting, of course he's going to come."

She's right. He will.

"Okay, let's review phase two," she says, handing me a piece of paper.

TOP SECRET MISSION
PARENT TRAP

PHASE TWO:
GET YOUR MUM OUT OF THE HOUSE

1.   *Plan a day out with your mum.*
2.   *When you wake up in the morning, look ill, but not too ill. (This shouldn't be too hard as you've been getting paler and paler since you got here. Just saying.)*
3.   *Pretend to be disappointed about missing the outing, but not too disappointed, else your mum will stay at home with you.*
4.   *As soon as your mum is out of the house, prepare a selection of sandwiches, maybe ham and cheese, unless your dad is vegetarian like your mum. If he is, maybe honey. Although maybe he won't want to eat honey because of the bee sting. Anyway, make some type of sandwiches. He will take the news better if he's not hungry.*
5.   *Feed Bear, Chickpea, Nestle, and Nugget. You'll probably forget later.*
6.   *Take Bear for a walk to tire him out. This might help you chill a bit. Plus, the plan will go better if Bear is asleep.*

7. *Practice what you're going to say to your dad when he arrives.*
8. *Rub your eyes to make them look red. Maybe slice an onion?*
9. *Put the kettle on. Tea is good for shock.*
10. *Text me updates.*
11. *Good luck!!!*

"Any questions about phase two?" Allie asks.

"No. What about phase three?"

"That's on you. I can't do everything. I did think about writing out different scenarios based on how your dad might react when he finds out you tricked him into coming to England, but I don't even know him, so . . ." Allie shrugs.

"So I just need to figure it out as I go?"

"Yes. I mean, you can text me and stuff, but I can't run operations from the other side of the world. If we had one of those dog cameras, I could at least monitor things. What was it called again?"

"The FurCam."

"That's it. Anyway, what's the worst-case scenario?"

"My parents hate me and get divorced."

Allie looks thoughtful.

"Yeah, that would be bad. Best-case scenario?"

"My parents understand why I did it, don't ground me

forever, and stay married, but happy married, not sad married."

"What's that thing about aiming for the stars and reaching the treetops? Maybe your parents will understand, ground you for a month, and stay married but unhappy."

"Do you think that might happen?"

"Maybe. But that would be better than them getting divorced, right?"

"I guess."

And I guess that makes me a really terrible person because when I think about it, when I really think about it, I want my parents to stay together, even if that does mean they aren't happy.

It's painful to watch Allie struggle with her packing, so I take over while she plays with Bear.

"Here," she says when I've finished. "I've got something for you. I was going to bring it on vacation, but you need it more." She hands me a book with a yellow cover titled *Think Like a Spy*. "You can't keep it, though—it's a library book. I've marked the pages you need to study."

I turn to the chapters Allie has stuck Post-its on.

"Covert Operations, Subtle Surveillance, Code-Cracking, Disguises . . . Disguises?"

"It's an interesting chapter. Plus, you never know."

"Allie, come on, the taxi's here," her mom calls from downstairs.

"Wait," I say. "I've got something for you." I reach into my bag and take out one of the crystals. "Here."

"What is it?"

"It's golden topaz. It made me think of you." I shrug, feeling embarrassed.

"Wow. It looks really expensive. I do still need the library book back, though. Sorry."

Allie glances around her bedroom as if she's looking for something else to give me.

"That's okay. I have loads of crystals. My friend Nora and I collect them. They're supposed to have different powers."

Allie smooths her thumb over the surface of the stone.

"You don't believe in all that stuff, do you?" she asks.

I shrug.

"Well, what powers is this one supposed to have?"

"It's a friendship stone," I tell her. "I've got a book all about crystals on the windowsill in my room. You can look it up in there if you want to know more about it."

"I don't believe in crystals, but I like it anyway. Thanks."

She puts the stone in her pocket, and my unexpected friend gives me an unexpected hug. I'm going to miss her. I don't know if I can go through with this without her. When Allie talks about the plan, something about the way she is so sure of everything makes me feel like maybe it could work. She makes it sound so easy. It's like her confidence is contagious, and instead of catching a cold, I'm catching courage. Allie is like a force of nature. She scoops up a problem, makes a snowball solution, rolls it down a mountain, and watches to see if it turns into an avalanche. Well, in this case, she won't be watching. She'll be five thousand miles away, but what choice do I have? I'm tired of doing nothing.

"I'd started to think they were never going to leave," Mom says as the taxi drives away. Bear watches it with a mournful expression on his face. "Now we can relax and enjoy our vacation. Just the two of us. Just like we'd planned."

Mom looks so happy that an icy wave of dread mixed with guilt with a side of anxiety washes over me. Things are about to get the exact opposite of relaxing, but with any luck, there'll be three of us, just like I'd planned.

I decide to FaceTime Nora and give her the lowdown on what's been going on since I got to England. We've texted and stuff, but she's been at surf camp most days, and I've been busy with Allie. Nora's eating her breakfast when she picks up.

"Hi," she says. I can just imagine her resting her

phone against the cereal box to talk. "How's England? Any more mystery relatives?"

"No, just the one. How's surf camp?"

"It's good. There's a cute English boy in my group. Are all English boys that cute?"

Nora has gotten boy crazy the last few months. It's annoying.

"I haven't seen any," I say. "Anyway, I wanted to talk to you about something important—you know that girl I told you about, Allie?"

"The one with the giant dog who wants to be a spy."

"Right, well, I told her I'm worried about Mom and Dad, and she came up with a really cool plan."

"A plan to do what?" Nora says.

And so I tell her.

"That is the absolute dumbest thing I've ever heard," Nora says when I've finished explaining the Parent Trap. "Nico! Come here. You've got to hear this."

Nico appears over Nora's shoulder, eating a piece of toast. "What's up?"

"Sage is going to try to trick her dad into flying to England by pretending her mom is sick."

"Why?"

"Because some English girl told her it was a good idea."

"It's not a bad idea," Nico says.

Nora hits him on the arm. "It's a terrible idea, you idiot. Don't encourage her."

"So what do you think I should do? I'm sick of doing nothing. I don't think Mom has even spoken to Dad since we got here."

"Why don't you just ask your mom what's going on? That's what we did," Nora says.

"Bad example," Nico says.

Nora scowls at him. "Well, it's a better idea than this dumb Parent Trap plan."

"I have to do something."

"Don't blame me when you're grounded for the rest of your life. Mom's yelling at us to go get in the car. We're late for surf camp, but I'll call you later. Don't do anything stupid!" Nora says, and the screen goes blank.

PART THREE

AWAY

CHAPTER NINETEEN

ALLIE
IS FINALLY IN CALIFORNIA

"Why do I have to share a room with Willow just because we're both girls? It's not fair." (from my diary)

The longest flight I've been on before this one was when we went on holiday to Greece. That took three and a half hours. It takes eleven hours to get to Los Angeles. Eleven hours! We got on the plane at four p.m. English time and landed at seven p.m. Los Angeles time, but according to Mum it's three a.m. at home. Does that make it today, tomorrow, or yesterday? As our taxi hurtles down a highway with twice as many lanes as the ones in England, I try to decide if I'm hungry or not. I've got this strange hungry/not hungry feeling. What meal would I even eat? It's like a math problem— if Allie gets on a plane in England at four p.m., eats some pasta at thirty thousand feet out of a little plastic tray before falling asleep while watching a movie, then wakes up and is given a sandwich, which may have been chicken or turkey, the flight attendant wasn't sure, and then arrives in a city where it's dinnertime, what meal should she eat?

I must have fallen asleep while trying to figure this out, as the next thing I know Mum is shaking my arm. I lift my head from her shoulder and wipe a bit of drool from the corner of my mouth. Gross.

"We're here," she says.

"This can't be the right place," I say, peering out of the taxi window at a big, ultramodern white house with a large shiny black door. It's like something out of a movie.

"Well, if it isn't the right place, then why is Willow hopping around on the front steps?" Mum asks, pointing and waving at my sister, who is clutching a squirming ball of white fur—presumably the antisocial Pandora. Dad and Max appear in the doorway behind Willow, and Dad pries Pandora from Willow's enthusiastic grasp and puts her down on the ground. The cat narrows her emerald eyes, gives Willow a death stare, and disappears into the house. I'm sure if Pandora could close the door behind her, she would. And she'd lock it.

Willow races over and flings herself at me.

"Allie, I lost a tooth. Look! Did Bear have his baby yet? Come and see our room. It's huge."

"Let Allie say hello to Dad and Max first," Mum says,

laughing. "Also, where's my hug?"

Willow barrels into Mum while I hug Dad.

"Aren't you going to say hi to your brother?" he asks.

"Hi, I guess," I say, scowling at Max.

I need to decide when and how to confront him about stealing my diary and showing it to Chloe Belton. But what if it was Willow who took the diary or Chloe Belton was just guessing about Toby, like Sage said?

"Hi," Max says, studying his shoes. Guilty people don't like to make eye contact.

"Okaaaaaay, then," Dad says. "Absence clearly didn't make the heart grow fonder for you two. Let's go inside."

We grab our bags and follow Dad up three steps and walk straight into a huge room that's the kitchen, living room, and dining room all in one. At the far end of the room is a wall of windows that reach from the floor to the ceiling. Through them, I can see the twinkling lights of what must be hundreds of houses stretching off into the distance—as if the stars had tumbled out of the sky.

"Oh, it's gorgeous!" Mum says, spinning around. "Now I feel terrible about Lauren and Sage staying at our place. Don't you, Angus?"

"Not really," Dad says cheerfully. "I'm just glad I get to stay here. Anyway, I thought Lauren told you she thinks our house is charming."

"Well, she did, but now I've seen where they live, I know she was just being polite."

"Where's all their stuff?" I ask.

Our house is overflowing with what Mum calls "knick-knacks," bought as souvenirs on vacations and days out over the years. I wonder what we'll end up bringing back from California. The only things on display in Sage's house are a couple of weird white sculptures on the mantelpiece, an enormous white candle on the table that has obviously never been lit, and a huge black-and-white photograph of Sage with her mum and dad, which is hanging above a futuristic-looking fireplace. In the photo, Sage is sitting with her parents on an enormous white sofa, and she has a bigger smile on her face than I've ever seen. The whole family is dressed head to toe in white. If I hadn't met Sage, I would suspect that her family is part of some weird cult.

Pandora, their on-brand white cat, pads across the pale wooden floor, glares at us, and heads up the stairs. If that cat sat on the sofa with her eyes closed, she'd disappear. I'll have to check the cushions before I sit down. I don't like cats, but I don't want to squash one.

"Come on, Allie, let's go to our room," Willow says, pulling on my arm.

"Our room?" I say, shaking her off and turning to

Mum and Dad. "You said I could have my own room."

"You can," Dad says. "Willow's missed you, that's all. You can sleep in the room next to hers."

"Is that Sage's room?" I ask.

"No, that's at the other end of the corridor."

"Great. That's where I'll be sleeping," I say, picking up my bag.

Willow sticks out her bottom lip. "But Dad, you said I wasn't allowed to sleep in Sage's room, and it's so pretty. I wanted to play with all her things. She's got all different colors of nail polish and some magic stones."

"That's exactly why you're not allowed in there," Dad says.

Maybe he's been thinking about the "Is My Child a Kleptomaniac?" article.

"Then Allie can't sleep in there either," Willow says in a sulky voice.

"Actually, Sage said it was fine for me to sleep in her room because we're friends, but nobody else is even allowed to go in there. Nobody."

I turn and follow Pandora up the stairs.

Sage's bedroom is perfect. The bed is so neatly made it looks like it's never even been slept in. Unlike downstairs, there are lots of interesting things on display. I walk over and study the bookcase first. The books are in alphabetical order, of course. On the bottom shelf is a collection of stuffed animals—bears, cats, dolphins, horses, llamas—oh my god, has Sage alphabetized her stuffed animals? It must be exhausting to be this organized. There is a row of bottles of nail polish of every color on another shelf with a gap where I suppose the silver polish usually lives, and there's a little metal tree with jewelry hanging from its branches. Sage really should not have left that out. I move the tree to a higher shelf, where Willow won't be able to reach it. She's bound to come in even though I told her not to.

I walk over to the window, drawn again by the view of the twinkling lights on the hillside. On the windowsill is a small display case half-filled with crystals, and next to it is a book called *Crystals A–Z*. I should probably hide the crystals from Willow too. I can't believe Sage and her friend waste their money on a bunch of rocks. I mean, they look pretty, but they could have bought a basic surveillance camera for that. What did Sage say the crystal she gave me was called? Golden topaz? I turn to the *G*s. There are two *G*s: galena and garnet. I try the *T*s. Tektite, thulite, tiger's-eye—here it is, topaz. There are six different colors. I run my finger down the page until I reach golden topaz.

Color: Golden Yellow
Chakra: Solar Plexus, Sacral (I have no idea what that means.)
Origin: Mexico, Japan, Brazil, Australia, Madagascar, Myanmar, Russia, Africa, Sri Lanka, USA
Meaning: The golden topaz promotes deep friendships and reminds you to value true friends. It's a fun, sunny crystal that brings a real sense of joy. Are you looking for a special gem for a true friend? If so, golden topaz might be the crystal for you.

Now I feel really bad about only having lent Sage my library book. I wonder if they sell *Think Like a Spy* in America. Maybe I could ask Mum and Dad to take me to a bookstore, and I could buy her a copy of her own. I'll even put it in the *T* section of her bookshelf.

In the shower, I try a bit of every potion and lotion I can find. I don't think Sage will mind. I mean, I don't care what she uses out of our bathroom at home. Mind you, we do only have the Elsa shampoo and conditioner, the lavender shower gel that Max always complains smells too girly, and the minty bath salts Mum uses when her back is playing up. I pat myself dry with an enormous white fluffy towel, wrap myself in a soft white robe, and dry my hair with a rose-pink towel with a clever button at the back to hold it in place. This is the life.

I decide to FaceTime Sage. I'm not 100 percent sure what time it is in England, but she picks up on the fifth ring.

"Allie?"

"Guess where I am right now? Your bedroom. I can't believe you have your own bathroom, lucky thing. Why didn't you tell me? I used your shampoo and shower gel and stuff. I hope that's okay. What time is it there? How's Bear?"

"It's early. Bear is asleep like I was."

Sage yawns, which makes me yawn.

"Sorry," I tell her.

"It's okay. So, I told Nora about the Parent Trap plan, and she said it was the dumbest idea she'd ever heard."

Rude! It can't be the dumbest idea she's ever heard. I mean, there were definitely parts of the plan that needed work, but it wasn't terrible.

"So, what great idea did your friend have?"

"She didn't. I told her I'm going ahead with our plan."

"You did? You are?" I ask her.

"Yes. Didn't you think I would?"

"Honestly? No."

"Why not?"

"Well, it is kind of extreme, and even if it works, you'll get into a ton of trouble."

"I don't care," she says, sounding more determined than I've ever heard her. "I've got to try."

"Okay, then," I say.

"Remember, you need to keep your phone on so I can tell you when to call Dad. Okay?" Sage says fiercely.

"Okay, okay."

"Good. I'll talk to you later."

"Good luck," I say. She's going to need it.

CHAPTER TWENTY

SAGE
IS PARENT TRAPPING

"Citrine is considered to be a crystal of abundance and good fortune. Do you need some extra luck in your life? If so, citrine might just be the perfect crystal for you." (from *Crystals A–Z*)

I smooth the cloudy pale yellow crystal with my thumb and think about what Allie said earlier. It was bad enough that Nora thought the plan was dumb, but now even Allie doesn't seem to think it will work. What should I do? Something or nothing? The crystal feels silky and warm in my hand.

"Sage, the cab's here," Mom calls up the stairs.

"Coming."

I take a deep breath, tuck the citrine carefully inside my pocket, and head downstairs. Something, I decide, definitely something.

The drive to Oxford takes an hour, and I'm not sure whether it's the car ride or nerves making me want to puke. Probably both. Mom keeps telling me I look pale, which I guess is a good thing because, in less than twenty-four hours, I need to convince her I'm sick—but not too sick.

"It says here that Oxford is known as the 'city of dreaming spires,'" Mom says, looking up from her guide-book. "We're going on a walking tour led by an Oxford university student, which ends with a punt down the river. Won't that be fun?" She beams at me. "It's like the first real day of our vacation."

I have no idea what a punt is or whether it'll be fun, but hopefully, it will help stop me worrying about the Par-ent Trap, which starts in—I look at my phone—six hours!

Punting turned out to be going slowly down a river in a boat while Giles, the student tour guide, pushed a pole against the bottom of the river to move us along. Giles said the word "punt" comes from a Latin word meaning "flat-bottomed boat." Mom said it's like going in a gon-dola, but Giles didn't look as if he agreed. I don't think he likes being a tour guide very much. He did cheer up when Mom tipped him at the end of the tour.

Back at the cottage, I wait until Mom goes to the bathroom and then grab her phone from her bag. Hope-fully, she won't notice it's missing until morning. I race upstairs, switch it off, and shove it under the Elsa pillow. Even if Mom does notice her phone is missing, there's no way she'll suspect me of taking it. I'd never do anything like that. Well, I never would have done. My heart is racing as if I'd just chased Allie across two and a half fields. Step one is complete. I head back downstairs.

"Have you seen my phone?" Mom asks, turning out the contents of her bag on the kitchen table.

I feel my face getting hot. "No. Maybe you left it in the taxi."

"Ugh," she says, searching through her stuff.

"I'll go feed the chickens while you look," I say and head for the door, trying not to feel too guilty about her sighs.

I ignore the chickens, who start clucking as soon as they see me—I'll feed them later—and head to the beehive on the other side of the house. Mom never comes near it. I check my phone, crossing my fingers that I still have Wi-Fi. My phone shows three bars. Now the difficult part. I need to call Dad. I'm not going to FaceTime him because I probably look really guilty. It's going to be hard enough to lie without having to look at him. Dad picks up on the third ring.

"Hey, honey. I was going to call you later. I had a—"

"—Dad, you have to come to England! Mom was stung

by a bee and had a really bad reaction."

"What? Is she okay?"

"No. She must have left her EpiPen at home. The doctors are doing all kinds of tests."

"You're at the hospital?" Dad asks.

"No, Mom is. I mean, I was there, but they said I should go home, so I came back to Cringle Cottage."

"On your own?" he says, sounding worried.

"Yes. In a taxi."

"Are Emma and Allie with you?"

"No, they're at our house. They left yesterday."

"So you're at the house alone?"

"Yes—well, no, Bear's here."

"Who?"

"Bear. The dog."

"You can't stay on your own, Sage. I'm going to call your mom to figure out what we should do, and then I'll call you right back. Okay?"

"Okay."

A minute later, he calls back.

"Mom's not picking up," he says.

I think about Mom's phone, safely turned off, currently being guarded by Elsa.

"I told you, she's having tests. She won't be able to pick up. I thought you couldn't have cell phones in hospitals.

Don't they interfere with the machines?"

Allie told me that. I'm not sure if it's true, but she said that it definitely is, and it sounds good. She said that details are essential in putting together a good cover story but that you should try to keep things simple at the same time.

"Don't deviate from the truth unless absolutely necessary," Allie had said firmly.

"But the whole thing is a lie."

"Obviously, but you should include things that actually happened. Like if you had scrambled eggs for breakfast, you should say that. It'll make you sound more believable."

"I had scrambled eggs for breakfast," I tell Dad.

"What?"

"Nothing," I mutter.

I need to get him off the phone before Mom comes looking for me.

"Um, I've got to go, Dad. There's someone at the door."

"You shouldn't be answering the door when you're there on your own," Dad says, sounding panicked.

"It's okay. I looked through the window. It's Mrs. Armstrong. She owns the village store. She's really nice."

"Well, can you stay with her until I figure out what we're going to do? I need to book a flight. Can you put her on the phone?"

I hear the back door of the house open. Shoot, Mom's coming.

"Dad, I've got to go. I'll get Mrs. Armstrong to call you."

I lean back against the nearest tree and let out an enormous breath.

"Sage," Mom calls from the doorway. "I'm going to get started on supper. Can I get some help?"

"Coming."

I trudge back toward the cottage, stopping to feed the chickens on the way. I can feel my heartbeat slowing down.

"I can't belieeeeeeeeeve you have to look after those disgusting creatures on your vacation. The Greenwoods should be paying you to stay there."

I cannot deal with Chloe Belton right now. I know people just like her at home—all fake-friendly to your face and then talking about you as soon as you're not around. Allie's the complete opposite of that. She's more likely to stick up for you behind your back and be rude to your face. I miss her.

"We don't mind," I say. "And they're not disgusting."

"Why did you even swap houses with them? Mrs. Armstrong told my mum that your house in California is super fancy and has a pool and everything."

I shrug, hoping Chloe will take the hint and go away. She doesn't.

"I reaaaaaaaaaaalllllly miss Luca," she says, sighing tragically.

"Who?" I ask, even though I know exactly who she's talking about.

"Luca," she says, flicking her hair. "My boyfriend. In Italy."

I smile to myself, thinking about what Allie said about him being fake. I bet she's right. Chloe scowls at me.

"What's so funny?" she asks.

"Nothing," I say. "You just reminded me of something Allie said."

"Poor Allie," Chloe says. "She's never going to get a boyfriend. I think Toby South likes me. Maybe I'll break up with Luca and date him instead." She twists a strand of her hair thoughtfully. "What do you think?"

I want to tell her I couldn't care less what she does, but instead, I just tell her I've got to go. I've got enough to worry about without fighting with Chloe Belton.

My stomach is churning at dinner, and I tell Mom I'm not hungry. I guess that's not a bad thing to say, as it will make it more believable when I say I'm sick tomorrow. Allie would approve. She says in the spying world it's called laying a trail of bread crumbs.

"I'm going to bed to read," I say. "I'll help you clear."

"Don't worry, honey. I'll do it. You look tired. I'm going to have an early night too. I'm really looking forward to tomorrow. Aren't you?"

I hug her and tell her I am, and that just makes me feel even worse.

As soon as I get to Allie's room, I check my phone. There are five missed calls from Dad and three texts.

Today 6:11 PM
I'm booking a flight.

Today 6:17 PM
The earliest flight I could get is at nine tonight. I land at Heathrow at 8:40 a.m. It's a couple of hours' drive to Little Moleswood, so I'll be there around eleven.

Today 6:18 PM
Okay????

Oh my god, Dad is actually coming. He's booked a flight. This is happening. I look around the room, not sure what I'm looking for, but I wish that Allie would magically appear and tell me things will be okay. The phone vibrates in my hand.

He answers before the first ring has finished.

"Thank God. I was worried. Did you see my texts?"

"Sorry, I was helping Mrs. Armstrong with something. So you'll be here tomorrow?"

"As long as there are no delays, I'll be with you by eleven. I still can't get hold of your mom. What's the number of the hospital?"

"The nurse gave me a card with the number on it. I'll find it and text it to you."

"Great. Where are you now?"

"I'm at Mrs. Armstrong's house."

"Can you put her on the phone?"

"She's in the garden, but I'll get her to call you back in a minute."

I really hope Dad doesn't ask why I don't just take the phone into the garden.

"Okay. Don't worry, honey. I'll be there tomorrow. Everything's going to be fine. Don't forget to text me the number of the hospital. I love you."

Phew! I hang up the phone and slump down on the bed, feeling exhausted and wide awake at the same time. Bear gives my face a friendly lick.

"Now we need to call Allie," I tell Bear. "I can't believe I'm actually doing this!"

Bear looks at me encouragingly, although what I really deserve is one of Pandora's death stares.

CHAPTER TWENTY-ONE

ALLIE
IS NOT HANGING TEN

"Why do we never do what I want to do? We take a vote, and I lose every single time. Mum and Dad say that it's a democracy, not a dictatorship." (from my diary)

I haven't got a clue what time it is when I wake up the next day. At least, I think it's the next day. I might have been asleep for a week. Sage's room is pitch-black, and the house is pin-drop quiet. I stretch out and make snow angels in the soft white sheets of the giant bed. It's so comfy. If it weren't for the fact that my stomach is growling like Bear does when he sees a rabbit, I'd probably just stay here. But the growling isn't stopping, so I get out of bed, my feet sinking into a sheepskin rug. No wonder Sage's mum kept commenting on all the sheep. She was probably wondering how many fleeces she could fit into her suitcase. I hold out my arms like a sleepwalker and head in what I think is the direction of the door.

"Morning, sweetie," Dad says when I get downstairs. "Did you have a good sleep?"

"What time is it?" I ask, squinting my eyes against the dazzling sunlight, which is flooding in through every window.

"Just after ten. Fancy some breakfast?"

"Yes, please. I'm starving. What time is it at home?"

"Six," Dad says.

I look at him, confused.

"In the evening," he adds.

Eeeeeeek! That means Sage will be talking to her dad soon. Maybe she already did. I check my phone. Nothing.

"Where's everyone else?" I ask.

"Mum's still asleep. I dropped Max and Willow off at surf camp."

"Surf camp?"

"Max and Willow started there yesterday. Here," he says, handing me a piece of paper.

SURF'S UP SUMMER CAMP
Monday–Friday | 9 AM–1 PM
All Skill Levels Welcome
Equipment Provided (Surfboard + Wet Suit)
All Instructors Have Water Safety & First Aid/
CPR/AED Certifications
EVERY DAY'S A GOOD DAY WHEN THE SURF'S UP!!!
www.surfsupsummercamp.com

Surf camp? That sounds absolutely hideous.

"They'll love that," I say, passing it back to him.

I can't believe my luck. With Max and Willow at surf camp, I might actually get to do some of the stuff that I want to do. Tomorrow we could go to that street where all the famous actors have their handprints in the sidewalk. I'm not sure if I'll be able to see their fingerprints, but I hope so. Then maybe the next day we can go shopping and I'll get some cool Californian back-to-school clothes. I can just imagine running into Toby on the first day, tanned and with golden highlights in my hair, which has somehow magically grown below my shoulders. His jaw would drop. He might even blush a tiny bit. "Hi, Allie," he'd say. "You look amazing." In this scenario, Chloe Belton has left the country, and Max has been sent away to boarding school. This is going to be the best vacation ever.

"Don't worry," Dad says, interrupting my daydream, "the instructor said it's okay for you to start tomorrow."

"What?"

"Brad said you can start tomorrow."

I look at him in horror. "Me? I'm not going!"

"Of course you are."

"I hate the sea," I tell him. "You know I do."

Dad frowns. "Do you?"

"Yes."

"Does she?" he asks Mum, who has just walked into the kitchen yawning widely.

"She's scared of fish," she says.

"It's not just the fish. It's all the other stuff," I say, frowning at her.

"Well, all the more reason to get used to it," Dad says. "You can't spend your life not going in the sea. Anyway, it's only four hours a day."

"But I don't want to go. It's supposed to be my vacation."

"It's everyone's vacation, and we're taking advantage of the unique opportunities here. Imagine how cool it will be to tell your friends that you learned to surf in LA! You can't do that in Little Moleswood, can you?"

"My friends won't think it's cool."

"Max said his friends would."

"Max and I have very different friends."

"It'll be fun," Mum says. "You'll meet a bunch of kids from California."

"I don't want to meet a bunch of kids from California. Besides, I already know Sage."

"Fine. Well, they have campers from all over the world, so maybe you'll meet some English kids." Dad sounds annoyed now.

"Why do I need to meet English kids? I go to school with three hundred and fifty of them."

"Allie, why do you always have to be so contrary? Your brother and sister were both excited to go, and you're going too. Majority rules. End of story."

"Majority rules sucks when the majority always wants to do the opposite of what I want to do. It's not fair. I'll just hang out here with you and Mum."

"Well, Mum and I won't be here, so you can't."

"Where will you be?"

"We're going to surf camp too. We can't let you kids have all the fun. Hang ten, dude!"

Dad makes a fist with his thumb and pinkie finger sticking out and waves his hand about in what I'm guessing is supposed to be some kind of surf thing. I didn't think surf camp could sound any worse, but the idea of my parents trying to act cool . . . ugh! I've only been awake for ten minutes, and my vacation is already ruined.

"I'm going outside," I say.

"What about your breakfast?" Dad asks. "I've toasted you a bagel."

"I've lost my appetite."

I slide open the glass doors and step out onto the terrace. Most of the garden is taken up by the pool, which has narrow strips of very dark green, almost fake-looking spiky grass around the sides. When I step on it, it hardly moves. I stomp down—nothing. On the bottom of the pool is a mosaic of tiny tiles, all different shades of blue, and a giant bright pink inflatable flamingo is bobbing on the surface of the water. It doesn't look very comfortable—you'd have to rest your head against its skinny neck to float around. I bet that Willow convinced Dad to get that for her—she's obsessed with flamingos. She'd better not be planning to bring that back to England. I'm not having that thing in my room.

I walk past the pool to the end of the garden. In the distance, I can see the ocean glimmering. I guess that's where Max and Willow are right now and where I'll be tomorrow if I can't think of a way to get out of it.

"Isn't it gorgeous?" Mum says, handing me the biggest bagel I have ever seen. "I wonder if Lauren and Sage think our view is as amazing."

"I doubt it," I say, taking a bite. I really am hungry. "Do I have to go to surf camp, Mum?"

"You do. You never know; you might even have fun."

I'm about to tell her that there is no way I'll have fun when my phone pings. I read the text from Sage. *CALL DAD IN FIVE MINS!!!*

"Who's texting you?" Mum asks. "Dad's going to kill you if you're running up a huge phone bill. He's already reminded me to turn roaming off three times."

"I'm on the Wi-Fi. I'm going inside. It's too hot out here."

I race up the stairs to Sage's room and look in the mirror. "Hello, dear," I say to my reflection. "I'm Gwen Armstrong." *Think Like a Spy* says you need to inhabit the world of your alias. I take a deep breath and dial the number Sage sent me.

"Hello?"

Sage gets her non-question questions from her dad.

"Hello, dear. This is Gwen Armstrong. Am I speaking with Sage's father?"

"Yes. This is Ethan Grayson. Thank you so much for calling."

Sage's dad sounds worried and relieved all at the same time. I feel a twinge of guilt.

"It's my pleasure, dear. Terrible news about the bee sting. Poor Lauren. Not to worry, I'll take excellent care of Sage."

"Thank you so much." Sage's dad lets out a deep sigh of relief. "So you'll keep Sage with you until I arrive tomorrow? I should be there around eleven."

"Yes, indeed. It will be my pleasure."

"I haven't been able to speak to Lauren yet. Can you tell me anything more about what happened?" he asks.

"Oooops, hold on a second, dear, there's someone at the door. I have to go. Don't you worry about a thing. Sage will be absolutely fine here with me, and we'll see you in the morning. Goodbye."

I hang up and text Sage right away: *MISSION ACCOMPLISHED!!!*

That was easy.

Max and Willow look tanned and happy, and they can't stop talking about the stupid surf camp when they get home. They're both wearing yellow T-shirts with pictures of surfboards on the front and Surf's Up Surf Camp written in white letters on the back. Max is wearing a ridiculous pair of swim shorts with garish tropical flowers on them that almost reach his knees, and—oh, it can't be. It is.

"Are you wearing a necklace?" I ask.

Max blushes and touches a brown beaded necklace.

"So what?" he says. "All the surfers wear them."

"That is so cringey."

"I have a necklace too, Allie. Look!" Willow says, holding up a necklace with a small white shell on it.

"Maybe we should all get surfer necklaces," Dad says.

"I will not be getting a surfer necklace because, as I've told you a thousand times, I'm not going to some dumb surf camp," I say.

Dad waves a piece of paper in my face until I snatch it off him.

"The instructor said you should read this."

"You're going to have so much fun," says Willow,

hopping from foot to foot. "I'm a Whitewater Warrior. Come and watch me do handstands, Allie. Max has been teaching me."

"Race you," Max says. He tears off his Surf's Up T-shirt and does a cannonball into the pool, soaking me from head to toe.

He definitely did that on purpose. I sit in the shade and watch as Willow does handstands. Max helps her by catching her legs. My ribs squeeze tight as I watch them laughing together. Everything is so easy for them.

"Come in, Allie," Willow shouts. "You can have a turn on Tutu McFeathers!"

"I only just got out of the pool," I lie and look at the piece of paper Dad gave me.

SURF'S UP SURF CAMP
BRAD'S AWESOME TIPS FOR NEWBIES

1. *Spend time on dry land practicing your pop-up.*
    (Perfect, because I plan to spend all my time on dry land.)
2. *Start small.*
    (I will not be starting.)
3. *Keep your feet moving to reduce the chance of being stung, etc.*

(What? What's the "etc."? A shark biting off your legs?)

4. *Work on your paddling technique.*
(I'm still stuck on tip three.)

5. *Get used to falling. Just remember that falling isn't failing!!!*
(Great.)

6. *Listen to your body.*
(My body is telling me not to go surfing.)

7. *Last but not least: HAVE FUN and HANG TEN!!!!!!*
(I will definitely not be having fun because, after reading these so-called tips, I am more determined than ever not to learn to surf.)

CHAPTER TWENTY-TWO

SAGE
IS AWAKE

"Pyrite, also known as fool's gold, is a powerful stone of protection and confidence. Are you facing a formidable challenge? If yes, pyrite is the crystal for you." (from *Crystals A–Z*)

"Morning, sleepyhead," Mom says when I walk into the kitchen, trying to look sick but not too sick.

I don't even have to try to look pale. I've been up half the night, my mind and my stomach churning with a mixture of panic, disbelief, and a tiny pinch of hope. When I finally got to sleep, I dreamed I was running through an airport trying to find Dad while a flock of sheep with enormous teeth chased me.

"Not dressed?" she asks in surprise.

"I don't feel good," I say in a raspy voice. "My throat hurts."

Mom reaches out and touches my forehead and cheeks.

"You don't have a fever," she says. "That's good."

"It hurts to swallow, though."

"How about I make you some honey-and-lemon tea

while you go and get dressed, and then we can head out. I'm really looking forward to seeing Blenheim Palace. It's supposed to be beautiful."

"I don't think I'm well enough to go," I say, trying to look disappointed—but not so disappointed that Mom decides she shouldn't visit the palace without me.

Her face falls.

"But you should go," I tell her. "I'll be fine. I'll just stay here."

"I can't leave you here on your own when you're not well. We can go to Blenheim Palace another day."

"I won't be on my own. I have Bear, and I can always walk to the shop to see Mrs. Armstrong if I need anything." I pause, swallow, and rub my throat, wincing. "Honestly, Mom, I'm not all that interested in seeing the palace."

"But I don't even have my cell phone," Mom says. "I've been looking for it everywhere. You'd have no way to reach me if there's an emergency."

"I'll be fine. I'm eleven. I can totally stay on my own for a few hours. I might just go and read upstairs. I'll take Bear with me."

Mom looks torn.

"We only have a few days left," I remind her.

I suck. Not only am I lying to Mom, I'm pretty much ruining her vacation. I hope she'll understand. I think back to her words to Nora and Nico's mom: "Maybe if we'd made more time for each other. Maybe then things would have been different."

"You should go," I repeat firmly. "I'll be fine."

CHAPTER TWENTY-THREE

ALLIE
IS ASLEEP

"I told my mum that I can't sleep because of Willow's snoring. Willow says I snore too, but I know for a fact that I don't." (from my diary)

ZZZZZZZZZZZZZZZZZZZZZZZZZZZZZZZZZZZZZZZZZZZZZZZZZZZZZZ

ZZZZZZZZZ

ZZZZZZZZZ

ZZZZZZZZZ

ZZZZZZZZZ

ZZZZZZZZZ

ZZZZZZZZZZZZZZZZZZZZZZZZZZZZZZZZZZZZZZZZZZZZZZZZZZZZZZZZZ

CHAPTER TWENTY-FOUR

ALLIE
IS AWAKE

"If Max calls me Cheeto Head one more time, I'm going to kill him." (from my diary)

As soon as I open my eyes, I check my phone. Yikes! That's a lot of texts.

Today 3:15 AM
Dad just got here. He's in the bathroom. He's going to be so mad. I think I might throw up.

Today 3:18 AM
He's still in there.

Today 3:19 AM
He's coming out!

Today 3:45 AM
Dad is SO MAD.
I have never seen him so mad.
I'm going to be grounded forever.

Today 4:12 AM

Dad's gone for a walk.

He told me to stay EXACTLY where I am.

He didn't want a sandwich or a cup of tea.

I told him he'd feel better if he wasn't hungry. He made this weird snorting sound.

Today 4:45 AM

HE'S BACK!!!

He cursed when I told him I hid Mom's phone. He NEVER curses.

I'm in SO MUCH TROUBLE.

Today 5:28 AM

He fell asleep.

Where are you???

Today 6:17 AM

He's awake and yelling again.

Mom is going to be back soon. SYGFHKSBE%$!!!!!

Oooops. I mean, I guess we could have seen that coming. I call Sage, but she's not picking up. Maybe her dad took her phone. Well, there's not much I can do to help her, so I may as well focus on my own issues: how to get out of going to surf camp. I have a plan.

"I don't feel well," I announce when I get downstairs. "I think I should stay here."

"Told you," Max says to my parents triumphantly.

"What?" I ask, glaring at him.

"I told Mum and Dad that you'd pretend to be ill so you wouldn't have to come to surf camp."

"Nobody asked you, Maximilian," I say, turning my back on him. "Mum, I think I got sunstroke yesterday. I should probably stay indoors. Did you read that article I emailed you last night?"

"Sorry, love, I didn't see it."

"Dad?" I ask.

"What?" he asks.

"Did you read the article about parenting a child with red hair?"

"No, did you send it to me?"

"Ugh!" I say, stamping my foot. "Why don't you ever pay attention? This is important." I pull up the article on my phone and read, "'As the parent of a redheaded child, it's essential to be aware of the risks of sun exposure. Redheads carry a gene called MC1R, which increases the risk of developing malignant melanoma. Children with red hair are less able to protect themselves against the sun's UV rays, with people carrying the MC1R gene showing additional sun damage equivalent to spending an extra twenty-one years in the sun.' An extra twenty-one years! Did you know that?"

"Very interesting," Mum says. "Well, luckily, you don't look at all sunburned from yesterday, so just make sure you wear plenty of sunscreen again today. Get some breakfast, and then go and get ready. We're leaving in half an hour."

The beach is crowded, which sucks because it means there are loads of people to see me looking like a complete idiot. Willow runs ahead to join a bunch of little kids doing cartwheels on the sand. She looks as if she's known them for her whole life. I wonder if I was ever like that when I was younger. If I ever just pranced up to a bunch of kids that I hardly knew and started doing cartwheels with them. I doubt it. I was never any good at cartwheels or meeting people.

I stand next to Mum and Dad, wearing a white sun hat with a flap of material that covers my neck, which Mum just bought in a store near the beach parking lot. Maybe she was paying attention when I read the article. She didn't buy Max or Willow a sun hat with a neck flap. I look like a complete dork, but I can't not wear it after the fuss I made about the MC1R gene.

A man with shoulder-length wavy blond hair, big muscles, and an even bigger smile walks over, gives Dad a high five, and then turns to me.

"G'day, mate! You must be Cheeto," he says in a strong Australian accent. "I'm Brad."

I blink at him. "Um, no, I'm Allie."

He looks over at Max. "Your brother told me everyone calls you Cheeto."

Max sniggers and wanders over to a group of teenagers, including a very pretty girl with dark curly hair. She's wearing a turquoise short-sleeve wet suit and a shell necklace like the one Willow has. Max keeps looking at her, but she's busy chatting with another girl and not paying any attention to my brother. Good for her.

"Well, they don't," I say. "Literally nobody calls me that except Max, and he's an idiot."

"Mind if I call you Cheeto?" Brad says. "It kind of suits you."

"Yes, I do mind," I say, but Brad is already clapping his hands to get everyone's attention.

"Okay, guys, join the groups you were with yesterday."

Please don't let me be in Brad's group. Please don't let me be in Brad's group. Please don't let me be in Brad's group. I cross my fingers behind my back.

"Hey, Cheeto! You're with me," he says.

I give Brad a death stare, which he doesn't seem to notice.

"It's Allie," I say between gritted teeth.

"Got it! So, Allie, because you missed yesterday's class, I'll whiz you through the basics, and then we'll figure out which group you should be in," he says. "Now, remember, guys, no peeing in the wet suits unless you're wearing your own!"

Willow blushes.

"Don't worry about it, Willow. It happens to the best of us. I try not to do it because the acid damages the neoprene, but . . ." Brad shrugs and grins.

"Do people really pee in their wet suits?" I mutter to myself.

"All the time," a boy next to me says. "That's why I have my own."

The boy has jet-black hair that sticks up on top like Chickpea's crest.

"Ugh, so you can pee in it?" I ask.

"No, so he knows nobody else has," says a girl standing on the other side of him. She has exactly the same color hair as the boy, but hers is in two buns on top of her head. Her hairstyle makes her look a bit like Minnie Mouse.

"Race you to the water, Nora," says the boy, and the two of them run off down the beach.

I didn't think I could have wanted to surf less than I did earlier, but I do now that I know I'm going to have to wear a wet suit that someone has probably peed in. I glare over at my parents, who've joined a group of adults. They're standing on surfboards on the sand, looking totally ridiculous. I hope someone has peed in their wet suits.

"Time to get suited up," Brad says to me.

"Um, I need to ask my parents something first. They're over there."

"Okay, but be quick. You don't want to miss out on surfing time, do you?"

I roll my eyes and start to trudge across the hot sand to where Mum and Dad are trying unsuccessfully to jump from a push-up position to standing.

"I need money," I say.

"What for?" Dad asks.

"To buy a wet suit."

"The instructor will give you one. You don't need to buy one. You borrow one. It's included," Dad says.

"I'm not wearing a wet suit that people have peed in," I say, looking my parents up and down and raising my eyebrows meaningfully.

"Who would pee in a wet suit?" Mum asks. "That's disgusting."

"I mean, if you're way out in the water and you need to pee, what do you think people do?" Dad says.

"See!" I say to Mum. "People like Dad pee in their wet suits—that's who."

Mum looks at Dad with narrowed eyes and curls her lip.

"That's disgusting, Angus, but no, Allie, we're not buying you a wet suit."

I stomp back over to Brad.

Getting the wet suit on, pee or no pee, is gross. It's almost impossible to pull it up, and the material drags on my skin. By the time I have it on, I'm hot and sweaty. My face is probably the same color as my hair, and I just want to go back to the house and call Sage. I wonder what's going on with her now. Her mum must be back. Whatever is going on, I'd rather be there than on this beach.

"Great," Brad says when I've finally struggled into it. "Getting the wet suit on is the toughest part. Let's run through some drills here on the sand and then get in the water."

"Today? I thought the first day we'd be practicing out of the water. Doing the jump-up thing."

"That only takes about ten minutes. Let's get going."

I manage to make the on-land part of the lesson last for forty-five minutes by taking a bathroom break (which I don't need), a hydration break, another bathroom break (which I do need), and then asking Brad loads of questions about his surfing career. People like talking about themselves. Once they get going, you don't even have to listen—just smile, nod, and look as if you're interested in what they're saying.

"Check me out blathering on about the good old days back in Oz," Brad says eventually. "Less talk, more action. Come on, let's go."

I take a couple of steps into the sea. I have to admit the water feels great on my feet, which are probably blistered from the burning sand. Brad shows me how to paddle out, which is way harder work than it looks. I practice paddling around for about ten minutes before Brad tells me it's time to "catch a wave." Max had been making jokes on the drive here about me not even being able to catch a cold. He thinks he's so funny. He's not.

There is no way I'm going to be able to stand up on this thing.

"Do I have to stand up?" I ask Brad.

"That's the plan."

"But those kids are lying down."

I point down the beach to where a group of kids are riding waves into shore, lying on their stomachs and laughing. They look to be having fun. They probably have their own wet suits.

"They're on bodyboards. You're learning to surf, remember? We'll do the four-step method, just like you practiced on the beach. When I tell you, get on all fours, put your left foot where your left knee was, your right leg inside your right hand, then stand. You've got this, girl!"

I do not have this, but I can tell that Brad isn't going to let me get out of the sea without me trying to catch at least one wave.

"Can I get out after this?"

"Sure. You ride one wave in, and you can get out if you want to, but I promise you won't want to. Let's go!"

I may as well get this over with, so I paddle reluctantly after Brad.

"Okay," he says. "This next wave is all you. Paddle!"

Back at the house, Max still hasn't stopped laughing.

"I bet you didn't get it on your first try," I say.

"Actually, I did," he says. "So did Willow."

Brad had, of course, been lying when he said I could get out of the ocean after one wave.

"I said you could get out after you've *ridden* one wave in," he said, smiling and pushing his long hair out of his eyes.

I spent the rest of the lesson falling off my surfboard, swallowing salt water, and generally hating my life. Eventually, Brad put me out of my misery and said I could get out.

"You did great," Brad said as I waited for the others to finish their lessons. "Remember, what is falling not?"

"Failing," I muttered.

"Right. Tomorrow you'll be riding waves like a pro. Hang ten!"

I didn't mention that I have absolutely no intention of being there tomorrow.

"Who's coming in the pool?" Mum asks when we get back to the house.

"Not me. My ear hurts. I'm going inside," I tell her.

"Hopefully, you'll feel better for the trip to Griffith Park," Dad says. "We're leaving at three."

I will feel better for this afternoon's outing because we're going to see the Hollywood sign and places where different movies were filmed. My ear can start hurting again on the way home.

As soon as I get inside, I check my phone, but there are no new messages from Sage. I wonder what's going on with her parents. I decide not to FaceTime her in case her mum or dad answers. Hopefully, Sage won't have thrown me under the bus, but you never know. Maybe things have calmed down, and she and her parents are having a laugh about the whole thing. Maybe they were impressed by her creativity. Maybe not.

CHAPTER TWENTY-FIVE

SAGE
IS IN A WORLD OF TROUBLE

"Peridot is a must-have crystal for anger management. Do you need to let go of negativity and resentment in your life? If so, peridot is the crystal for you." (from *Crystals A–Z*)

The silence is even worse than the yelling. I wonder if I could sneak my peridot crystal into Dad's pocket. I study him across the kitchen table. He's gazing at his hands, and every few minutes, he looks right at me, sighs, shakes his head, and then looks back down at his hands.

"I just don't understand why you did it, Sage. It's not like you to lie. You stole your mom's phone, pretended that she was sick and in the hospital, scared me to death, and had me fly halfway across the world. Why? Why would you do that?"

I shrug, determined not to start crying again.

"I told you I don't want to talk about it until Mom gets here," I say, looking at the table and swallowing hard.

"Oh, really! You don't want to talk about it! And what

do you think Mom is going to say about all of this when she does get here?"

A car door slams outside the cottage, and Bear barks and trots toward the front door. I guess we're about to find out. Another wave of nausea washes over me, and I want to run. I want to run out of the back door, past the Chick-Inn, climb over the wall, and just keep running through the fields until I'm so far away from the cottage that nobody will be able to find me. I feel the tears prickling painfully and close my eyes. This is going to be so bad.

"Hi, honey," Mom calls from the hallway. "The palace was amazing. I wish you'd seen it. How are you feeling?" She comes into the kitchen and stops in her tracks. "Ethan! What on earth are you doing here?" Mom looks back and forth between Dad and me.

"You should ask our daughter that question," he says.

"I don't understand." Mom turns to me. "Sage?"

I do the only thing I can do—I burst into tears. Mom hurries around the table and puts her hand gently on my shoulder. She rubs my back like she did when I was a little kid and couldn't fall asleep. "What's the matter, honey? What happened?"

I cover my eyes and don't say anything.

"Ethan, will you please tell me what you're doing here?"

"For some unknown reason," Dad says, his voice ominously calm, "Sage called me yesterday and informed me that you had been stung by a bee and were in the hospital. I panicked and got on the next available flight to London. I even spoke to some weird-sounding woman who told me that Sage could stay with her overnight until I arrived."

I peek at my parents through my fingers. Mom's face is scrunched up with the effort of trying to make sense of anything Dad just said.

"What? What are you talking about? Which woman?" Mom asks.

"The woman who owns the store in the village," Dad says.

"Mrs. Armstrong? You spoke to Mrs. Armstrong? This doesn't make any sense."

"I agree. It makes no sense at all! Anyway, whoever I spoke to told me you were in the hospital and that Sage could stay the night at her house."

"But I was here last night," Mom says, shaking her head as if she can make the puzzle pieces fall into place. "I haven't been to the hospital. I didn't get stung."

Dad sighs and runs his fingers through his hair. "I know that now, Lauren! Sage, crying isn't going to help. How about you start explaining what on earth this is all about."

I look up at my parents. Mom is staring at me like I've got two heads, and Dad looks madder than ever.

"I just thought . . ." My voice trails off. "I just thought . . ."

"You just thought what?" Dad yells.

"Let her talk, Ethan. She's obviously upset," Mom says, putting a hand on his arm.

"She's upset? *She's* upset? I'm probably going to lose the contract in New York. I literally dropped everything to come here. I've been frantic."

"Calm down," Mom says.

"Calm down? Are you serious?" Dad says, standing up. "I was worried about you, Lauren, and I thought our eleven-year-old daughter was on her own in a strange country and being looked after by some random woman."

"I don't understand how Mrs. Armstrong is involved in all of this," Mom says. "Also, Mrs. Armstrong is nice."

Dad sighs impatiently. "Lauren, I don't care who Mrs. Armstrong is or whether she's nice or not. I want to know why I am sitting here in the middle of nowhere when I should be at work in New York."

"Sit down, Ethan. This isn't helping. Sage, why don't you tell us what's been going on, honey."

"I just thought . . ."

My voice comes out all squeaky. Mom passes me

a tissue, and I blow my nose loudly. She passes me another one.

"I just thought that if we could all be together on vacation, you might, well, you might be happy again."

Mom and Dad exchange glances.

"What do you mean?" Dad asks.

"Well, everything's been weird at home for ages, and then Mom said we were coming to England without you, and I heard Mom talking on the phone to Kristen, and she said that maybe if you guys had more time, then . . ."

"Then what?" Dad asks, looking at Mom, who shrugs.

"Sage?" she says.

I gulp. "The last time I can remember you guys being happy, like really happy, was last summer on vacation. I thought maybe if we were away from everything, you might remember that you love each other, and maybe you wouldn't . . ." My voice cracks, and I put my head back into my hands. I don't want to say the words.

"Wouldn't what, honey?" Mom says.

"Wouldn't get divorced." I sigh the words into my hands.

"Oh, Sage," she says. "Why didn't you talk to us?"

"I did. I asked you why we couldn't all just go on vacation together, and you lied and said it was because Dad had to work."

"I did have to work," he says. "I do have to work."

"But we could have gone on vacation another time. I'm not stupid. You treat me like a baby and like there's nothing wrong. Well, everything is wrong. I know it is."

I stand up, shoving my chair back so that it makes an angry scraping sound on the tiles, and run out of the kitchen, out of the back door, past the Chick-Inn, climb over the wall, and keep running across two and a half fields. I run faster than I've ever run. Nobody is quick enough to see my legs disappear underneath the thorny bush. Nobody will find me here.

CHAPTER TWENTY-SIX

ALLIE
IS CODING

*"We saw an actual Enigma machine at
Bletchley Park today. The sign said it has
158,962,555,217,826,360,000 different settings.
Cool."* (from my diary)

The next morning when I check my phone, there is
still nothing from Sage, which is weird. I decide to
call her, even though her mum or dad might answer. Her
phone goes straight to voice mail. I don't leave a message. I'll text her instead—something innocent-looking
that could mean I had nothing to do with the whole stolen phone/fake illness/flight from New York to England/
impersonation of Mrs. Armstrong, etc. It does sound bad
when I put it like that.

Sage and I should have agreed on a secret code for our
messages before I left England. *Think Like a Spy* has six
fairly easy ones I could have taught her. My favorite is
the Bump and Shift method. You bump the last letter of
each word to the first letter of the next and then shift the
spacing to the left by one. For an extra level of security,

I usually add a 1 at the beginning of the word and a 0 at the end. It should be obvious to Sage that she needs to look at the Cipher chapter in *Think Like a Spy*—if she can't figure that out, there's no hope.

1AR0 1EYOU0 1RMU0 1MAN0 1DDA0 1DGETTIN0 1GA0 1DIVORC0 1E0?

Okay, that is terrible. I may as well just write "divorce" in all caps. Anybody could crack that code, even if they'd never heard of the Bump and Shift cipher. I need a different word for "divorce." I know.

1AR0 1EYOU0 1RMU0 1MAN0 1DDA0 1DBREAKIN0 1GUP0?

Better, but "breaking up" stands out too much. The longer the word, the less well this code works. I'll try again.

1DI0 1DYOU0 1RMU0 1MAN0 1DDA0 1DSPLI0 1TUP0?

Okay. Send.

CHAPTER TWENTY-SEVEN

SAGE
IS LOST AND FOUND

"Sodalite is the perfect crystal to enhance your communication skills. Do you know what you want to say but can't find the right words? If yes, sodalite may be the crystal for you." (from *Crystals A–Z*)

The soft light is beginning to fade. I wonder if I'm brave enough to stay out here all night. Allie would be. The scratches on my arms are stinging, but nowhere near as much as the ones on my heart. I don't need Mom and Dad to tell me what's going to happen. I know. I've known all along. I'm stupid for thinking I could change anything. Stupid for trying. Stupid for hoping. Stupid.

I should probably head back before it gets dark. Allie said my parents would call the police if I ran away, and she's right. I know I should go back to the cottage, but my entire body feels heavy, like I don't have the energy to wriggle out from underneath this bush, walk across two and a half fields on my own, climb over the wall at the end of the garden, and go back into the cottage. I don't even have the energy to be me.

"Woof, woof, woof." Bear's distinctive deep bark echoes across the fields. He sounds far away. I wonder if Allie trained him as a sniffer dog. It wouldn't surprise me. Did my mom or dad give Bear my sweater to smell and ask him to find me?

"Sage! Sage!" Dad's voice sounds even farther away than Bear's barking did. I wonder if Mom is with him or if she went in the opposite direction. Maybe she ran into the village to see if Mrs. Armstrong or Reverend Stella had seen me. Mrs. Armstrong is probably organizing a search party. I really should go back.

"Sage!" Dad calls, his voice sounding closer.

Bear's barks are coming from right outside the bush now, and I can hear him scrabbling around. His nose appears through the branches, then disappears, and he starts barking again. If Bear could speak human, he would 100 percent be saying, "I found her! She's here. Do I get a treat?"

"There you are," Dad says in a soft voice, pulling a couple of branches apart and peering in. He'll have scratches all over his hands. "Come out, honey."

I shake my head.

"I'm just going to sit down here and wait until you're ready to come out," says Dad.

I don't reply. It seems like a very long time since I sat

next to this bush, waiting for Allie to come out.

"Ethan, did you find her?" Mom shouts.

Dad must point at the bush, because the next thing I know, Mom is crawling in. She crawls through the branches until she reaches me and strokes my hair back from my wet cheeks. I didn't even know I was crying until I felt her touch.

"Sage," she says, hugging me so tight it hurts. "Don't ever run off like that."

"Is there room for me in there?" Dad asks.

"Not really," Mom says.

"Ouch!" Dad's face appears. "Come out, or else I'm coming all the way in, and it's looking kind of crowded."

Mom looks at me and raises her eyebrows. I sigh and wriggle my way out while Dad holds the branches up. Bear greets me by licking my face. He's wagging his tail so hard that his whole body is shaking. He's the only one enjoying this. Dad carefully pulls twigs and thorns from my T-shirt and hair before wrapping me in a giant hug. I rest my face against his soft shirt and breathe in and out. I can almost feel our heartbeats slowing down.

"How about we go back to the cottage?" he says into my hair.

Mom dusts herself off and takes hold of one hand, and Dad takes the other, and we walk back across the two and a half fields. Bear runs around us, drawing circles around my little triangle family.

"So it was Allie pretending to be Mrs. Armstrong on the phone?" Mom asks as she hands me a steaming bowl of pasta. "Why am I not surprised?"

"It's not her fault," I say. "She was just trying to help."

I look at Mom and Dad sitting across the table from each other. This wasn't exactly the dinner I was hoping they'd have on Dad's first night here. No candles, no champagne, no laughter; just red eyes, exhausted expressions, and slumped shoulders.

"You really need to eat something, honey," says Dad.

I twirl spaghetti around my fork, but I don't put it into my mouth. I set my fork down and look at my parents.

"I'm sorry," I say. "I didn't know what else to do."

"How about we talk about all of this in the morning? Everyone's exhausted," Mom says.

"You're breaking up, aren't you?" I blurt out.

Mom sighs and looks at Dad, who gives her a small nod.

"We were going to tell you when we got back from vacation. We didn't want to ruin your whole summer. Dad had to go to New York with work anyway, so rather than tell you and then have Dad go away for a couple of weeks, we thought it would be better to talk to you when we got back; then we could both be there to help you process things. I'm so sorry, Sage."

"We were trying to tell you in the best way we could think of. I guess we messed that up." Dad takes a deep breath. "Mom and I have decided we need some time apart."

"You mean more time apart than just this vacation?" I ask, even though I already know the answer.

"Yes," Mom says in a soft voice, reaching out to take my hand. "More time than just this vacation. When we get home, Dad's moving out."

Dad reaches over and takes my other hand.

"Where to?" I ask, trying to swallow the boulder-size lump that's sticking in my throat.

"I found a condo a few blocks from Nora and Nico's house," he says. "It's nice. You'll like it."

"Near their mom's house, or their dad's house?" I ask him bitterly.

"Their mom's."

"Nora and Nico's parents hate each other. Do you hate each other?"

"Your dad and I could never hate each other, Sage. We just don't think us living together is the best idea right now."

"Right now? You mean this might be a temporary thing—like a trial separation?" I feel a flutter of hope in my chest, like a baby bird testing out its wings.

Mom and Dad exchange glances.

"It's late, sweetie. Time for bed. We'll talk more in the morning," Dad says.

I guess that answers that question. The wings go still.

CHAPTER TWENTY-EIGHT

ALLIE
IS IN A WORLD OF PAIN

"I wish I was an only child." (from my diary)

own at the beach, the waves look even bigger than they did yesterday. Despite my having given what I thought was a realistic portrayal of someone with a severe ear infection, Mum and Dad said that I had to come back to surf camp. If I did have an ear infection, surfing would probably lead to a ruptured eardrum. Then they'd be sorry.

Everyone else in my family seems to be living their best lives on this vacation. I am not. I wonder yet again if I'm adopted. If my real, red-haired family is on vacation right now. I'm the only child in my imaginary family, so I pretty much get to choose what we do. That's the kind of family I should be in. Instead, here I am at the beach with my alleged real family. We're going on a hop-on-hop-off bus tour of Los Angeles after surf camp, so at least I'll finally see the street with the famous handprints. If my family doesn't hop off there with me, I'm getting off on my own.

After wriggling into my probably peed-in wet suit, I

skulk over to join Brad and the rest of the group.

"G'day, mate! You're with the Whitewater Warriors today."

"With Willow's group?" I ask, horrified.

"Yes, they might be groms, but some of them are pretty great."

"Groms?"

"Yeah, short for grommets. It's what we call the little-kid surfers. They're good, though."

I know they are. That's what I'm worried about—I'm going to look like even more of a loser falling off in front of a bunch of little kids. One of them has probably learned how to do a cartwheel on their surfboard by now.

"Yay, Allie," Willow says as she gallops past me into the water, hair streaming behind her, surfboard tucked under one arm. "You're a Whitewater Warrior just like me."

"Yay," I mutter.

After an hour of face-planting and swallowing half the ocean, Brad agrees I can go in to use the bathroom. I can tell I'm getting on his nerves by asking so often, but for all he knows, I might have bladder issues.

"Do you want to go with your sister, Willow?"

Willow giggles, so I am 99 percent sure that she just peed in her wet suit—probably while she was bobbing around next to me.

I drag my board behind me through the shallow

water. I guess having it tied to my ankle is useful for something, although it makes me scared the board is going to hit me on the head every time I fall off. Brad said that's why they give beginners the softer boards, which hardly hurt if they smack you in the face. I don't believe that it would hardly hurt to be smacked in the face by any type of surfboard.

I feel almost cheerful as I step out of the surf. It's not like Brad is going to come and check on me. I can easily stay out of the water for the rest of the lesson. Woo-hoo! OUCH! I unfasten the Velcro strap around my ankle and limp gingerly up the beach. I must have stepped on some glass. The sole of my foot feels like it's on fire. I sit down on my towel and examine it—weirdly, there's no cut, but lots of thin purple wavy lines are appearing on the sole of my foot, and it burns more and more each second—not like the burning of the hot sand, though: more of a prickly, buzzing feeling.

"Hey," Brad says, appearing with my abandoned surfboard under one arm and followed by a crocodile of Whitewater Warriors. "Are you okay?"

"I've hurt my foot. I stepped on something," I say, rubbing my eyes roughly to stop the tears I can feel welling up. It really does hurt.

Willow sits down next to me on the sand and pats me on the arm while Brad examines my foot.

"Thought so," he says. "Jellyfish sting—I saw a couple in the water earlier."

Knowing a jellyfish has stung me makes me start to cry for real. Through my tears, I glare at Brad. It's pretty irresponsible of him to let a bunch of kids go out into the ocean when he's seen dangerous creatures lurking in the water.

"It hurts," I say, knowing I sound like a little kid, but I don't care. "My foot feels like it's on fire."

"Let's get you to the lifeguard's tower," Brad says. "They'll have some tweezers."

"Tweezers?"

"Just in case there are any tentacles stuck in there."

"Tentacles? I think I'm going to throw up," I say, shuddering and putting a hand over my mouth.

"You're good. We'll have you right in a jiffy," says Brad in an annoyingly cheerful voice.

Brad tells the Whitewater Warriors to go and wait with one of the other instructors, but Willow refuses to leave me. Resting one hand on Brad's arm and the other on Willow's head, I manage to hop up the beach.

"Jellyfish?" the lifeguard asks.

Oh my god! If everyone knew there were jellyfish, shouldn't they have closed the beach or something? Or at least put up a warning sign?

"I'll go get the tweezers and a hot towel," she says.

"Lucky for you, we don't pee on jellyfish stings any-more," Brad says, laughing.

"People used to do that?" I ask.

"Yup, but don't worry, no pee involved these days! Once we've got any tentacles out with the tweezers, we'll press a hot towel on your foot. You'll be right as rain."

"But my foot's burning! I don't want a hot towel. I need ice on it."

"You might feel like you need to ice it," Brad says, "but it will make it hurt more, believe me. The heat slows the spread of the venom."

Now he's said "venom," I can practically feel the poison traveling through my foot, up my leg, and heading straight for my heart. I wonder how many people die from jellyfish stings each year. I lie back weakly.

One of the Whitewater Warriors appears, holding a shovel in front of her. On it is a gray lumpy thing.

"I found it," she shouts excitedly, waving her shovel at us. "Look!"

"I don't want to see," I say, turning away.

"Was it dead when you found it?" Brad asks, examining the jellyfish closely.

"It wasn't moving," the girl says. "Did Willow's sister kill it?"

I might kill her if she doesn't stop waving that jelly-fish in my face.

"I doubt it," Brad says, laughing. "Dead jellyfish can still sting."

"They can? You learn something new every day," Dad says, joining the group. Mum and Max are right behind him. Great! All I needed to make me feel even worse was my brother.

"Are you okay?" Mum says, bending down to look at my foot.

"What happened?" Max asks.

"Allie was stung by a jellyfish," Brad says.

"Poor jellyfish," Max says and walks away.

The only upside of my jellyfish sting is that my parents and Brad agree I should stay out of the water for the rest of the lesson.

"But back in tomorrow," Mum says.

"We'll be done in an hour," Dad says. "You relax here."

I think it's completely lame of my parents not to take me home immediately, but the lifeguard told them it wasn't a bad sting. Easy for her to say, given she's not the one with the swollen, purple-striped foot, so here I am, my burning foot resting on my surfboard, waiting.

Willow and the other Whitewater Warriors are taking turns riding on Brad's surfboard with him. Willow's suggestion that they re-create scenes from *Lilo & Stitch*, with Brad playing Stitch, was enthusiastically received at the beginning of the lesson this morning by all of the Whitewater Warriors apart from me.

I look farther down the beach to where Max's group, the Carving Crew, which sounds like the name of a school woodworking club, is clustered together like a pod of dolphins. I can see Max right away because his wet suit, much to my amusement and his horror, has fluorescent pink stripes down the arms. I hate to admit it, but he is excellent. Typical. Max and Willow seem to be good at all sports. I watch as my brother pops up like a pro and rides wave after wave into shore. How does he make it look so easy when I know for a fact it is practically impossible? Things that are difficult should look difficult. Max is going to be so annoying about this when we get home, particularly as I still haven't managed to stand up on my surfboard apart from on the beach. The instructor must have told the Carving Crew that it's time to get out of the water as, one by one, they surf gracefully to shore. Great, now maybe we can finally leave.

I stand up, ready to wriggle out of this gross wet suit, hopefully for the last time, and gingerly put some weight on my stung foot. It prickles as if I had stepped on a thousand nettles. Maybe I should sit down and wait for Mum or Dad to come and help me. I watch as Max rides in on an enormous wave. He's halfway into shore when he suddenly barrels forward, nose-diving off the front of the board. Ha! Now that he's wiped out, perhaps he'll stop showing off. I wait for him to reappear so that he'll know I saw him wipe out, but as the surf breaks, there's no sign of my brother, only his board rushing toward the beach.

CHAPTER TWENTY-NINE

SAGE
IS TALKING

"Larimar is an ideal crystal for anyone struggling to communicate how they truly feel. Do you need to vocalize issues close to your heart? If yes, this could be the crystal for you." (from *Crystals A–Z*)

1DI0 1DYOU0 1RMU0 1MAN0 1DDA0 1DSPLI0 1TUP0?

I study the text from Allie. I have no clue what it means and can't be bothered to figure it out. Last night while I lay awake, I practiced saying things like, "I'll be at my dad's house this weekend," and "I wanted to wear my pink sweatpants, but I must have left them at Mom's."

I wonder what's going to happen to Pandora. Will she be like me and move between the two houses, or will she live with Mom? Mom is Pandora's favorite. Dad pretends he doesn't like cats, but I've heard him talking to Pandora when he doesn't know I'm there. She hates going in her basket, so she won't want to move every couple of days like I'm going to have to. Thinking about Pandora makes my heart hurt even more. I try and fail to swallow the lump that seems permanently stuck in my throat and head downstairs.

Mom is setting the table for breakfast. There are three glasses, three bowls, and three plates. I guess from now on, all our tables will only be set for two. I feel another wave of loneliness crash over me at the thought of it, and the lump in my throat gets even bigger. Mom wraps me in a huge hug, and, as she holds me in her arms, we silently agree not to talk about anything important like how our family is broken until Dad is here. Instead, we work together to build a Leaning Tower of Waffles and put bowls of fresh strawberries and blackberries on the table, along with some wafer-thin slices of banana and a pot of honey we found in the cupboard labeled *Beeyoncé's Best*. I go out into the garden with Bear; feed Nestle, Nugget, and Chickpea; and pick some small purple flowers to put on the table. Mrs. Greenwood told me the flower is called knapweed.

"One man's weed is another man's wildflower," she had said, smiling when I'd asked her what it was. I had been planning on decorating the table with it for Mom and Dad's romantic dinner.

"Pretty," Mom says, smiling at the flowers. "Can you go upstairs and let Dad know that breakfast is ready? He's in—"

"—Max's room," I finish and wonder again about the

guest rooms at home. I suppose I needed to set my alarm earlier, or maybe Dad was sleeping in his office. I didn't even think of that. It doesn't matter now.

As I head for the stairs, I hear the now familiar creak of the top step, and Dad appears.

"Morning, sweetie."

I study his face to see if he is still mad, but he just looks sad. Sad and exhausted. He gives me a faint smile. I give him a small smile in return. It's the biggest one I have right now.

"Morning, Lauren," he says as Mom hands him a cup of coffee.

"Good morning. Let's eat, and then we can have a chat," says Mom.

We do our best to eat, but the Leaning Tower of Waffles only goes down by a couple of layers.

"Are dogs allowed to eat waffles?" Dad asks, looking at Bear, who is gazing at the pile of waffles and drooling.

"He probably shouldn't," Mom says. "Bear had some stomach issues. That's why Emma and Allie were still here when we arrived."

"Ah, the infamous Allie," Dad says. "I'm looking forward to meeting her one day. Also, the mysterious Mrs. Armstrong."

"Well, Allie is in California, but we can walk into the village and introduce you to Mrs. Armstrong later,"

Mom says. "Who, as we've established, had nothing to do with you being here, Ethan."

They both look at me. We all know we're dancing around the topic. People call it the elephant in the room, but this is more like a scorpion or a tarantula in the corner.

"So," says Mom, looking at Dad, "where should we start?"

"Is one of you having an affair?" I ask quietly, not looking at either of them.

"No!" they both say.

"Why would you say that?" Dad asks.

I shrug. I don't tell them what Allie said about 20 percent of divorces being due to cheating.

"Then why don't you love each other anymore?" I ask. If they don't love someone else, why can't they just go back to loving each other?

"We both love you very much," Mom says.

"And we care about each other," Dad says. "We always will. We share the best thing in the world—you."

"Nora and Nico's parents share them, and they can't even be in the same room as each other," I say bitterly.

"We're not Nora and Nico's parents," Mom says. "Not all divorces are like that. Lots of people manage to stay friends."

"For the sake of the children," I say.

Mom looks at Dad. "And for the sake of each other."

"It takes work," Dad says. "We know that."

I sigh and look down at Bear, who is resting his heavy head on my lap and gazing up at the waffles.

"We're sorry we didn't handle it better," Dad says. "We should have noticed how worried you were. I guess we've been too busy trying to protect you."

"We really didn't do a good job of that, did we?" Mom asks.

I shake my head.

"We probably made it worse," Dad says.

I shrug.

"Oh, honey, Dad and I hate the idea of you worrying and not feeling you could talk to us about it. I mean, the responsibility was ours to tell you, not yours to have to ask us."

"I was scared to ask," I admit. "I kind of didn't want to know. So I guess that means I knew all along."

I don't know how to explain to my parents that putting it into words would have meant it was happening. That somehow, if I didn't say it out loud, if nobody said the words aloud, then the cracks might vanish, and my family wouldn't shatter into pieces.

"Kind of like an ostrich," says Dad. "I get it. Your mom and I both stuck our heads in the sand for a long time too."

"You did?"

Mom nods and takes my hand. "It's scary to say the things you don't want to be true out loud. How about this: How about we all agree to say the important things, even if they're scary?"

"*Especially* if they're scary," Dad says, taking my other hand in his.

CHAPTER THIRTY

ALLIE
IS FRANTIC

"If Max is the oldest, and Willow is the cutest, I guess that makes me the nothingest." (from my diary)

don't realize I'm running until I'm waist-deep in the surf, the waves crashing into me, almost knocking me off my feet. I hear the piercing screech of whistles, and two lifeguards sprint past me and dive into the water, their red rescue tubes trailing in their wake. Their golden arms cut through the water effortlessly as they plow through the waves, which seem even bigger than they were just minutes ago.

"My brother," I try to scream, wading farther into the ocean, but my throat has closed up, and the words get stuck somewhere between my head and my mouth.

Someone grabs me from behind and picks me up. I struggle to get free.

"Allie, it's me," Brad shouts in my ear, pulling me back toward the beach. "It's Brad."

"I can't see Max! His board's there." I point at the surfboard, which is bobbing near the shore—the waves washing it in and out. "He fell off. I can't see him any-more." I'm sobbing now, taking big gulps of air. "Can you see him? Where is he?"

"Stay here," Brad tells me, shoving me toward some-one who takes hold of my arm firmly. "Keep hold of her," Brad yells and races off into the surf.

I scan the water with blurring eyes. Where is he? Where's my brother? The noise of the waves crashing mixes with the sound of my heart pounding in my ears until I can't tell them apart. Where is he?

"Look! They've got him! Look!" the woman holding me yells, her voice cutting through the chaos.

The two lifeguards are swimming on their backs, one arm each around my brother. A small crowd has gath-ered as the lifeguards reach the shore and carry Max a little way up the beach.

"Stand back!" Brad shouts, clearing a path for the lifeguards. "Give them space."

I break free of the woman holding my arm and run to Brad. The lifeguards roll Max onto his side, and another two lifeguards race up carrying a big bag. All the argu-ments I've ever had with my brother whiz through my mind—all of them pointless and stupid.

"What's happening?" I ask, desperately trying to see around the kneeling lifeguards. "What are they doing to him?"

"They're putting a neck brace on him in case he hit his head," Brad says calmly.

"He hit his head?"

"We don't know, but it's standard procedure if he's unconscious and they suspect a head injury."

"He's unconscious? Shouldn't you help?" I ask Brad. "Why aren't you helping?" I feel furious. Angry with Brad, my parents, Max, most of all with myself.

"Allie, they've got this. They're experts," Brad says, but I yank myself out of his grasp and run toward my brother.

"You're all right," one of the lifeguards is saying to Max. "We've got you. Just relax."

Max begins to cough and splutter. Foamy water trickles out of his nose and mouth. I race over and fling myself down on the sand next to him.

"Max. It's me."

Max opens his eyes, then barfs half the ocean all over my knees.

Brad goes to find Mum and Dad, who have been blissfully unaware of the near-drowning of their firstborn child. When they see Max lying on a board with a neck brace on and Brad explains what happened, Mum bursts into tears, and Dad looks as if he is about to do the same.

"We've called an ambulance," says one of the lifeguards. "It'll be here soon. That's a nasty cut. He'll need stitches, and he lost consciousness, so they'll want to monitor him at the hospital."

"Angus, I'll go with Max in the ambulance. You bring the girls in the car," Mum says.

"I'm not leaving my brother," I say. "I'm going in the ambulance."

I stick my chin out, and Mum and Dad look at each other. I hope they know that they'll have to pick me up and carry me off this beach if they think I'm leaving Max.

"Fine," Dad says. "We'll meet you at the hospital."

As the paramedics load Max into the ambulance, I look back at the beach. It's busy with people laughing, playing, surfing, and swimming, and it hits me like a ton of bricks that today, if things had turned out differently, I could have been leaving the beach without a brother. My vision goes blurry, and I see tiny black dots floating around. I try to blink them away, but I can't. Mum is saying my name from far, far away, then I feel my legs turning to jelly, and everything goes dark.

"Only Allie could make my nearly drowning about her," Max says when we are back at the house, but he doesn't sound snarky, just very, very tired.

He has a white dressing on his forehead where the

surfboard hit him. So much for Brad's claim that the softer boards don't hurt you. Tell that to my brother and his seven stitches, Brad!

The hospital we went to was super fancy. The white-and-gray marble floors and pillars in the entrance made it look more like a hotel lobby than a hospital. Max had an actual plastic surgeon do his stitches. Mum tried to make a joke about the surgeon giving her a quick face-lift when he'd finished with Max. The doctor didn't laugh but hopefully put her inappropriate humor down to shock. I tried to.

The doctor checked to see if I had a concussion because I'd hit my head when I fainted. They didn't do a test for embarrassment, which I was practically dying of when the medics insisted that I follow my brother into the ER sitting in a wheelchair. Willow wanted to ride in a wheelchair too, but everyone ignored her for once, and miraculously she shut up.

Nobody has the energy to cook when we get back to the house, so we order pizza. For once, Willow doesn't argue about what type to get. Even she seems exhausted. She shovels down a slice without complaining that it isn't Hawaiian. That's the one thing Willow always loses the family vote on—nobody else likes pineapple on their pizza, so Mum keeps some cans of pineapple in the cupboard at home so Willow can cover her pizza with it. Heaven forbid Willow does not get what Willow wants.

After dinner, Willow curls up next to Max on the sofa, sucking her thumb, which I haven't seen her do for ages. I'm tempted to tell her to stop it, that she's going to make her teeth wonky, but she looks so peaceful I decide not to. If she could read better, I'd email her an article tomorrow about the impact of thumb-sucking on mouth and teeth development, but she can't, and she doesn't have an email address.

Willow pulls her thumb out of her mouth with a popping sound.

"What was it like when you were under the water, Max? Were you scared?"

"It was like being inside a washing machine," he says. "I didn't know which way was up."

Max laughs when he says it, so Willow does too, but I can tell by his voice that he doesn't think it was funny.

"I'd have been scared," I say. "I'd probably have peed in my wet suit."

Max looks at me in surprise.

"I pee in my wet suit all the time," Willow says.

"We know," Mum says.

Dad yawns. "Well, I think we should all have an early night. I know I need one."

"I agree," Mum says, standing up and starting to clear the table. "It's the last day of surf camp tomorrow, and then we need to get packed. It's going to be a busy day."

I look at Mum. "You're joking, right? You don't seriously think we should go to surf camp after what happened to Max."

"I want to go," Willow says, pouting. "I want to surf, and I want to say goodbye to the Whitewater Warriors, and Brad said that on your last day, you get a little silver trophy shaped like a surfboard. I want a little silver surfboard trophy."

"Well, you don't get to decide because you're six," I tell her. "Mum and Dad decide because they are supposed to be adults. They're supposed to make sensible decisions."

"Calm down, Allie," Dad says. "Let's just go to bed. We can talk about surf camp tomorrow."

"I want my trophy," says Willow, pouting.

"Oh, shut up, Willow. The world doesn't revolve around you," I tell her.

Willow's bottom lip trembles, and her eyes fill with oh-so-easy tears.

"Allie, that's enough," Mum says. "The world doesn't revolve around you either."

"Oh, I know that!" I yell, heat rushing to my face.

"You didn't even see what happened to Max. You weren't even there. Max could have died, and you wouldn't even have known."

Mum slams the plate she was in the process of clearing back onto the table.

"Allegra," she says in a tight voice, "go to the kitchen. Now!"

I don't point out that the kitchen is, in fact, in this room. I just sigh and follow her.

"Yes," I say, scowling at her. "Did you want to talk about why going back to the beach where one of your children nearly drowned today might just be a terrible idea?"

"I am so sick of your snarky comments," Mum says in an ominously quiet voice. "You make it perfectly clear that you think we're terrible parents, and sometimes it's funny, but not today. Not today. You act as if we don't care about what happened to your brother or what could happen to any of you. Well, you couldn't be more wrong."

Mum's face is red, and she's slamming the plates into the dishwasher so hard that I'm surprised she hasn't broken one. She stops, plate in hand, and looks at me.

"You know what, Allegra, when you have kids of your own, you can do it your way. I don't need parenting advice from you, and don't you dare question whether Dad or I care. Don't you dare."

Mum storms out of the room. I wait until I hear her bedroom door slam before running upstairs and flinging myself onto Sage's bed, waiting for angry tears that never come.

I'm in exactly the same position ten minutes later, when Dad comes in. I'll bet he went to see Mum first.

"You've upset your mother," he says.

"She upset me."

"Today has been rough on all of us."

"Mostly Max," I say.

"Yes, mostly Max, of course, mostly Max." Dad sighs and rubs his forehead. "When you have kids of your own, Allie—"

"—if I have kids of my own."

"Fine. If you have kids of your own, you'll know that them being hurt, physically or emotionally, is the absolute worst thing in the world. I remember Mum saying when your appendix burst how she wished it could be happening to her instead of you."

I think about that day and remember Mum's pale, frantic face as she drove from the doctor's office to the hospital after telling him she thought she could get there faster than an ambulance. I hadn't even realized how much my stomach hurt until I saw her face.

"Let's talk more tomorrow. You need to get some sleep. We all do. I love you, Allie. Your mum and I both love you very much."

Dad closes the door softly behind him, and the tears that have been hiding all evening flow down my cheeks and soak into Sage's pristine pillowcase.

CHAPTER THIRTY-ONE

SAGE
IS WISER

"Azurite is a crystal of clear understanding and brand-new perspectives. If you need to examine the past and face the future with fresh eyes, then azurite might just be the crystal for you." (from Crystals A–Z)

For some reason, even though I know for sure that the thing I've been dreading for months is actually going to happen, I feel lighter. I can breathe more easily, and the knot I've had in my stomach has loosened, softly picked apart by my parents' gentle words and hugs.

I'll call Allie later and tell her what happened. I bet she'll think the mission was a success. I can just imagine her saying to me, "Sage, the Parent Trap worked perfectly because **ONE**, you got your dad to fly across the world, which is pretty impressive, given **TWO**, you've probably never even told your parents a white lie before, and **THREE**, now you actually know the truth, which, **FOUR**, was kind of the whole point, even though **FIVE**, your parents are still getting divorced, so **SIX**, you didn't really change anything at all."

But at least I did something.

Mom and I take Dad into the village to show him the sights—not that there are many, but he loves all the old cottages with roses climbing around their brightly painted doors and the ancient church.

"And here's the store. Bear, sit." I tie his leash to the bench, and he looks up at me mournfully. "He's not allowed inside because he stole a sausage roll from the counter," I explain to Dad, patting Bear on the head.

The now familiar jingling of the bell over the door announces our arrival.

"Hello. And who do we have here?" says Mrs. Armstrong from behind the counter.

"This is my dad."

"Hi," Dad says, stretching out his hand to shake Mrs. Armstrong's. "I'm Ethan."

Mrs. Armstrong looks shocked to have missed such a major development in Little Moleswood but quickly recovers, fluffs her white curls, and flutters her eyelashes at Dad.

"How lovely to meet you, Ethan. Lauren and Sage never told me you look like that gorgeous doctor from *Code Blue*. It's my favorite show. I never miss an episode."

Dad smiles at Mrs. Armstrong nervously. "Actually, I'm an architect."

"Well, you're handsome enough to be an actor," she says. "And it's a shame you're not a doctor, because my stomach's been bothering me. Anyway, I'm glad you managed to join your girls on holiday. I know they've been missing you. Did you decide to fly over to surprise them?"

Dad looks at me. "Not exactly. It's a long story. Sage here persuaded me that Little Moleswood was too special to miss."

"Well," Mrs. Armstrong says, fluttering her eyelashes again. "We certainly like it." She turns to Mom and me. "By the way, I never did ask you what was in that suitcase Derek found up at Moleswood House."

"It belonged to Violet's sister, Lily. We didn't even know Violet had a sister until we visited Reverend Stella! Her name was in the front of one of the books," Mom tells her. "There were some old photos, a couple of books, and some papers inside—mostly things to do with the house, copies of official documents and things like that. We haven't had a chance to have a really good look through everything yet. There's been a lot going on. Hasn't there, Sage?"

That's an understatement.

"What were the books?" Mrs. Armstrong asks.

"Dictionaries," I say.

"Why the heck would anyone keep dictionaries locked away in a suitcase?" Mrs. Armstrong says.

"That's exactly what Allie said when we found them!" I tell her.

"I'm surprised Allie didn't have you checking the dictionaries for secret messages. Did she tell you she used to get me to give her any old lemons I had to make invisible ink? She said to read a letter written in invisible ink, you have to hold it up to the light. Apparently, if you were caught with lemon juice during the war, you could be arrested—so Allie told me anyway. The things that girl knows. Anyway, I can't stand here chatting all day. I've got a cake in the oven. Come back in about an hour if you fancy some of my famous Victoria sponge."

Back at the cottage, I think about what Mrs. Armstrong said about Allie and invisible ink and decide to take a closer look at the dictionaries. I find a small flashlight at the back of the "everything" drawer. I open the *A–L* dictionary first and carefully flip through the pages, shining the light, searching for hidden messages, but nothing. Halfway through the *M–Z* dictionary, the pages are a lot more crumpled. I turn a few more pages, then drop the flashlight in surprise. There is a small gap cut out in the pages, and squeezed into the space is a little package wrapped in midnight-blue velvet fabric.

Holding my breath, I carefully pry it out and open it. Nestled on the velvety fabric is a large gold coin with a small bright blue globe in the center.

"Mom, Dad, come here!"

"What is it, honey?" Dad says.

"Look what I found."

My parents lean over to inspect the coin.

"Goodness, where did you find that?" Mom asks.

"In the dictionary. I was looking for messages in invisible ink and found this inside a hole cut out of the pages."

"Wow! What does that writing say?" Dad asks.

I read the inscription around the edge: "'G C & C S BLETCHLEY PARK AND ITS OUTSTATIONS.'" I turn it over to examine the other side and realize it's not a coin at all; it's some kind of medal with a pin to attach it to your clothes. On the back are the words *WE ALSO SERVED.*

"Bletchley Park," Mom says. "How extraordinary. That's the place Allie told us about, isn't it?"

"What's Bletchley Park?" Dad asks.

"It's where the codebreakers worked during World War Two," Mom says. "It's a museum now. It was number one on Allie's list of things to do while we're here."

"What was number two?" Dad asks.

"There wasn't a number two. She's a weird kid," Mom says.

I trace the words on the back of the medal with my finger. *WE ALSO SERVED*.

"Allie's not weird. I wish she were here right now. She'd be so excited. Maybe Lily worked at Bletchley Park during the war. Maybe she was one of the actual code-breakers."

"I can't believe that this was hidden inside a dictionary all this time," Mom says, shaking her head. "I wonder why Lily put it there."

"Can I take it to show Mrs. Armstrong?" I ask. "If she hadn't said that thing about invisible ink, I would never have even looked through the dictionaries."

"Of course you can," Mom says. "Can you imagine what Grandma is going to say when we show her? Be careful with it."

"I will," I say, wrapping the brooch back into its velvet bed and tucking it gently into my pocket. "I will."

"How wonderful," Mrs. Armstrong says, studying the medal. "I remember reading something about Bletchley Park in the local newspaper a while ago. What was it, now?" She gazes out of the window for a minute, deep in thought. "That's it! A woman in Great Moleswood worked at Bletchley Park during the war. There was an interview with her in the paper because she'd just got her telegram from the king."

"The king?"

"Yes. He sends you a telegram on your one hundredth birthday. I've only got thirty-seven years to go."

"Do you remember the woman's name?" I ask.

"I think it was Betty something. My friend Janice works in the pub up there. Let me give her a call."

Mrs. Armstrong takes a long time on the phone. When she finally bustles back through to the front of the shop, her cheeks are flushed, and she's grinning from ear to ear.

"I knew it was a Betty," she says triumphantly. "Betty Braithwaite. I just spoke to her on the phone. She's invited you and your parents for tea today. Here's the address. Why don't you take the Victoria sponge with you? I won't give you any of my homemade toffee; it might pull Betty's dentures out. Reverend Stella lost a filling last week!"

Betty Braithwaite lives with her daughter in a small cottage in the center of Great Moleswood, which looks identical to Little Moleswood except it's on the top of a hill. From the living room window, I can see the spire of St. Agatha's Church in the distance. I try to find Cringle Cottage, but nearly all of the houses in the village have identical honey-colored tiled roofs, and it's too far away to spot the little red roof of the Chick-Inn.

Betty Braithwaite is a tiny lady with a long silver braid hanging over her shoulder. Even though it's sunny outside—the sun has shone ever since Dad arrived— she's wearing a thick pale blue woolen scarf. She has silver wire-framed glasses, and the brightest blue eyes I have ever seen are studying me from behind them. Something about this old lady reminds me of Allie.

"Thank you so much for inviting us," Mom says. "Did Mrs. Armstrong tell you about the suitcase we found belonging to Lily Thornton?"

"She did," Betty says, smiling. "Lily Thornton, now, there's a name from the past!"

"Did you know Violet too?" I ask. "She was my great-great-grandmother."

"I met Violet a few times, at dances they held at the air base nearby. She was a nurse. It was Lily I knew well, though. We worked together at Bletchley Park."

"How did you come to be working there?" Dad asks. "It sounds like a fascinating place."

"I'd just joined the women's navy—Wrens, they called us—and during training, they gave us IQ tests and puzzles to do. I was always good at word games. Anyway, the next thing I knew, I was being given a train ticket to Bletchley Park and signing the Official Secrets Act. Churchill called us the geese that laid the golden eggs and never cackled!"

"Mum didn't tell anyone she'd worked at Bletchley Park for years," Betty's daughter says, setting down a tea tray with Mrs. Armstrong's cake in pride of place. "Did you, Mum?"

"I wasn't allowed to—it was all top secret. I wish my parents could have known what I did in the war. They'd have been so proud. Thirty years is an awfully long time to keep a secret." Betty gazes out of the window and sighs. "We worked hard, but we had some fun too. Hand me that photo album, dear. I think I have some pictures of Lily in there."

I pass her a large green leather album and perch on the arm of her chair as she turns the pages. In one of the photographs, a group of seven girls is standing in front of a big house.

"That's me," says Betty, pointing at a grinning girl at the center of the picture.

"You all look so young," Mom says.

"It was my nineteenth birthday that day," Betty says, smiling. "The girls made a cake for me. They all chipped in some of their sugar rations. Look, there's Lily."

Betty points to a pretty girl standing next to her in the picture. Lily is gazing straight at the camera with a broad smile on her heart-shaped face.

Betty turns to me and touches my cheek. "You look like her, dear," she says. "Lily and I lost touch after the war. It was a chaotic time. I moved down to London as soon as the war ended. I only came back to the area after my husband died. I did try to track Lily down."

"Why do you think Lily kept her medal hidden in a dictionary?" I ask.

Betty Braithwaite chuckles.

"She loved puzzles. She probably did it so that just the right person would find it at just the right time." Betty's eyes twinkle. "Knowing Lily, I bet she hid it under 's' for secret!"

Betty's daughter touches her arm gently. "Maybe it's time for a bit of a rest, Mum."

"I don't need a rest," Betty says. "Well, maybe I'll just close my eyes for ten minutes." She winks at me. "It was lovely to meet you."

"Would it be okay if my friend Allie came to visit you?" I ask. "She's in America right now, but she lives in Little Moleswood. She'd love to meet you. Bletchley Park is her favorite place in the world. She wants to be a spy when she's older."

"Does she, now?" Betty says, patting my hand and smiling. "Well, you tell your friend that she's welcome to visit anytime, and make sure you come and see me next time you're in England, won't you? We can go to Bletchley Park—I'll show you both around."

CHAPTER THIRTY-TWO

ALLIE
IS GOING HOME

"People always say that there's no such thing as a normal family, which makes mine normal in at least one way." (from my diary)

"Morning," Mum says when I walk into the kitchen. I didn't sleep well, and I'm guessing she didn't either, as she has dark circles under her eyes and her bedhead is even wilder than usual.

"Morning," I say cautiously. "Is Max up?"

"Not yet. He's still fast asleep. Allie, we should talk about last night before your brother and sister come down," Mum says.

"I'm sorry," I say, and I am. "I don't really think you and Dad are terrible parents."

"That's nice to hear," Dad says.

Mum studies me. "We know you were really upset about what happened to Max at the beach yesterday, but is there something else going on?"

"What do you mean?" I ask.

"You just seem so cross all the time. Like you think

that the world is against you," Dad says.

I look at him in surprise. I was expecting to get into trouble for being rude, but it's like they're talking about something else.

"I don't know what you mean."

"Oh, Allie," Mum says gently. "You just don't seem very happy, that's all."

"You mean since my diary got stolen?" I ask, feeling a hot flare of anger and like I might cry at the same time.

"Before that too," Dad says. "You know you can talk to us about anything. Why don't you try telling us what's going on? It might make you feel better."

An image of Sage's face pops into my head. All the times that I told her just to say what she needed to say to her parents. Not to be afraid. She was brave enough to get her dad all the way from New York to have a real, true, scary conversation with her parents. It turns out I'm the one who needs to be brave.

"Allie?" Mum says.

I take a deep breath, close my eyes, and when I exhale, the words spill out like water from a burst pipe.

"It's just that Max and Willow get all the attention. I mean, Max is perfect at everything—school, sports, friends, everything is easy for him. Then Willow came along, and her, well, her being her, and needing everything all the time and everyone thinking she's so cute even when she's being a complete brat, it was like I just disappeared. It feels like I don't matter as much as them. Like I don't matter at all."

Mum and Dad look at each other.

I blink away the hot tears brimming in my eyes. "And you and Max and Willow all like doing the same things together, and they're things I hate, like surf camp and roller coasters, and superhero movies, and it's like I don't belong in our family. Like you'd be better off without me. Like you'd have more fun without me."

"Oh, sweetie! Of course you matter. Of course you belong. You're just so independent. Isn't she, Angus? Max always needs driving to and from swim practice, and cricket matches, and parties, and Willow always needs, well, Willow things."

"You've always been like that," says Dad. "You've wanted to leave home since you were five, you've known which university you want to go to since you were six, and you decided on a career when you were seven. You're just so, so . . ."

"Capable," Mum says.

Dad nods. "Exactly. What is it Mrs. Armstrong always used to say about Allie when she was little? Four going on forty."

"But I'm not forty. I'm a kid." And right now, I feel closer to four, and the tears finally begin to roll down my cheeks.

"Why is Allie crying?" Willow asks, skipping into the room dragging the inflatable flamingo with her. "Allie never cries."

I rub my eyes roughly and turn my back on my sister.

"She's just feeling a bit sad," Dad says.

"I'm sad too," Willow says. "I'm sad because you said you didn't know if I'll be able to bring Tutu McFeathers back to England with me, and she really wants to come. She'll share a room with Allie and me, and she'll sleep in my bed every single night."

"Um, Willow," Mum says. "Can you give us a minute, please? We're in the middle of an important conversation with your sister right now."

"But I need to be in the middle of an important conversation about Tutu McFeathers right now."

"Here, take my phone. You can play on it upstairs for ten minutes," Dad tells her.

Willow, Tutu McFeathers, and Dad's phone disappear up the stairs in a flash.

Mum comes over and hugs me. "I'm so sorry, honey. I'm so sorry we ever made you feel that way."

"I just want to be as important as everyone else."

"Allie, you are! Of course you are," Dad says.

"But I don't feel like I am. I want you to listen to me

when I tell you that I hate tomatoes."

"You hate tomatoes?" Dad asks.

"You knew that, Angus," Mum says. "Didn't you?"

Dad shrugs apologetically. "Did I?"

"And having a vote for everything we do isn't fair when I like different things than Max and Willow."

Mum and Dad look at each other.

"It always seemed the fairest way, given there are three of you," Mum says.

"Maybe it's the easiest way. Not the fairest," Dad says, looking thoughtful. "I'm sorry, love. I never thought of it that way. We can change that. What else?"

Half an hour later, Mum, Dad, and I have made a list of six things we could do differently as a family. **ONE**, we will take it in turns to choose a movie and what kind of takeout we're going to have on Friday evenings, but **TWO**, nobody—including me—is allowed to sulk about what the other person chooses, else **THREE**, the sulker will skip their turn, and **FOUR**, we'll have a weekly family meeting from now on—the first agenda item will be this list—so **FIVE**, we are going to have to actually listen to one another, which is going to be practically impossible for our family, which is why **SIX**, I came up with the idea of us getting a talking stick to make sure we do.

They aren't the biggest things in the world, and I'll still have to sit in the middle seat in the car and share a room with Willow, but it's a start.

When Max comes down for breakfast, he looks so much better—almost back to normal if it weren't for the bandage on his head. I shudder, remembering the moment at the beach when I realized if things had been even a tiny bit different—a bigger wave, a harder hit, a slower lifeguard—I might have left the beach without a brother. Max might not be sitting opposite me right now, chewing toast in a gross way. I smile at him and pat his arm awkwardly.

"What's up with you?" he asks, spraying crumbs all over the table. "Why are you being so weird? Get off me!"

"I think Allie is just pleased to see you," Dad says.

I blush, and Max shrugs.

"What time are we leaving?" he asks through a mouthful of toast.

"You can't go in the water, Max," Mum says. "You know that."

"I know, but I still want to go and say goodbye to everyone."

"I was planning on staying here with you and Allie while Dad takes Willow to camp," Mum says.

I look up at her in surprise. I was sure my parents

would make me go to surf camp.

"I'll stay with them, Emma," Dad says. "You're better at surfing than me anyway."

"I want to say goodbye to my friends and thank you to the lifeguards," Max says quietly while Mum and Dad discuss who should go surfing and Willow prattles on about wanting to bring Tutu McFeathers with her and tiny silver surfboard trophies.

"Why don't we all go?" I say. "That way, Max can say goodbye to his friends and thank you to the lifeguards; you, Dad, and Willow can surf, and I'll, well, I'll wait for you all."

"Are you sure, honey?" Mum asks.

"I'm sure."

"Okay, be ready to leave in thirty minutes," Dad says. "And thank you, Allie. That's very considerate of you."

Mum grins at me.

"I told you she was being weird," Max says.

I smile and head upstairs to get ready for the beach. Give-and-take feels way better than get-mad-and-get-even.

I study my reflection in the heart-shaped mirror in Sage's bedroom as I apply sunscreen. The mirror has tiny lights around the edge. I'm thinking about Sage looking at her heart-shaped face in her heart-shaped mirror when my phone rings. I pick up and there's Sage, sitting in my bedroom.

"Sage! I've called you like a gazillion times! What's been happening? Are you grounded forever? I thought maybe your parents had confiscated your phone."

"I am pretty much grounded forever, but Mom said I could keep my phone in case I wanted to talk to Nora about—well, stuff."

"Stuff?"

"You were right. They were waiting until Mom and I got back from England to tell me."

"They're breaking up?"

"Yes. Dad's moving out when we get home," she says in a small voice.

"I'm really sorry. About the plan and, well, everything."

"It's okay. You were right. It is better to know than not know. I mean, I guess I knew anyway. I just wanted it to go away." She sighs. "Anyway, what's going on there?"

"Not much," I say. It doesn't seem the right time to tell her about Max nearly drowning and my talk with my parents. Maybe I'll tell her another day. "How's Bear?"

"He's good. How's Pandora?"

"I woke up the other day, and she was sitting on your desk staring at me. It was super creepy. I think she misses you. How's great-great-whatever-her-name is? Any more long-lost relatives?"

Sage's face lights up. "You are never going to believe what happened yesterday."

And she tells me all about a hidden compartment in the dictionary—why didn't I think of that?—the Bletchley Park medal, and meeting an actual codebreaker. Who would have thought Sage's boring school project would lead to my favorite place in the world? Who would have thought there was an actual codebreaker living in Great Moleswood? Who would have thought that Little Moleswood could be more exciting than LA? Also, there are no jellyfish in Little Moleswood, and nobody's likely to drown in the duck pond. I'm ready to go home.

Down at the beach, everything looks exactly as it did yesterday morning, but nothing feels the same. Willow chases off to cartwheel with the Whitewater Warriors and pull on her peed-in wet suit for the last time, Dad heads off for his final surfing lesson, and Mum sits down with Max and me.

"You should surf, Mum," Max says. "I would if I could."

"Would you really?" I ask. "Even after what happened yesterday?"

"One hundred percent. I love it. You go, Mum."

"Are you sure?" Mum says. "I'll come and check on you in a little while. Allie, make sure your brother doesn't go in the water."

She hurries off to join Dad and the rest of the Swell Seniors or Offshore Oldies or whatever their group is called.

"Are you okay?" Max asks.

"Yeah, why?"

"You and Mum really got into it last night. Were you in trouble this morning?"

I shrug. "I said sorry."

"And that was it?"

"Pretty much."

Max will find out about the family meetings and the talking stick soon enough.

"Hey," Brad says, strolling over and kneeling on the sand to study Max's head. "How are you feeling, mate? You gave us all quite a scare. I had to stop Allie from diving in to rescue you."

"My head feels okay. Mum and Dad said I'm not allowed to go surfing, though," Max says.

"Absolutely not!" Brad says. "Even I'd stay out of the water for a while after taking a surfboard to the head. Any stitches?"

"Seven," I say, glaring at Brad.

"How about you, Allie? Fancy a last try at catching a wave?" Brad asks, either not noticing or ignoring my scowl.

"No thanks."

Brad shrugs. "Okay, well, I'm going in. See you later."

Max and I sit in silence for a while, watching the Whitewater Warriors. Willow's getting really good. I must have inherited my athletic ability from Dad, who has just face-planted for the third time in ten minutes. Unlike me, Dad comes up laughing and looks like he is having the time of his life. Max's friends from the Carving Crew come over to say hi, and I don't even tease him when Maya, the girl with the beautiful hair, takes a selfie with him, texts it to him so he has her number, and gives him a brown leather braided bracelet. I wonder if she thinks it will remind him of her hair. I don't think my brother will have any problem remembering Maya. He'll probably spend the next year telling anyone who'll listen about his hot Californian girlfriend. Even though she's not his girlfriend, at least Maya's real, unlike Chloe Belton's Italian boyfriend.

"You should go in, Allie," Max says when the Carving Crew has gone back into the water.

"Um. That would be a hard no," I say.

"Why not? I watched you yesterday. You were getting better. Seriously, Allie, you won't get another chance, and if you don't try again today, you never will. I know what you're like—you'll tell everyone it's because I almost drowned, but really it's because you're scared."

I glare at Max, but to my surprise, he doesn't have a

mean look on his face.

"It's okay," he says. "I'm scared of stupid stuff too."

"Like what?"

He shrugs.

"Tell me!"

"No, it's dumb. You'll tell everyone."

"I won't," I say.

"Promise?"

"Promise."

"Okay, I'll tell you what I'm most scared of if you go in and surf, just for a bit."

I look at Max. I guess I could get him to tell me the secret and then not go into the water. What's he going to do about that?

"I know what you're thinking," he says.

"I'm not thinking anything," I say, trying to hide a smile.

"Yeah, you are. You're thinking, *I'll get Max to tell me what he's scared of, and then I won't go surfing.*"

"I wasn't thinking that!"

He raises an eyebrow at me, and we both laugh.

"Fine, I was thinking that."

"Seriously, Allie, go in, then I'll tell you."

"No way. I'll go in, swallow a gallon of water, step on another jellyfish, then you won't tell me! Plus, I'm supposed to stay here with you."

I'd forgotten all about the jellyfish sting. I bend my leg to examine the sole of my foot. There are still faint purple wavy lines on it, but it doesn't hurt anymore. I wonder if the lines will always be there. Max has his bracelet from a cute surfer girl, Willow has Tutu McFeathers, and my souvenir of our trip to California will be the scars from the venom of a dead jellyfish.

"Look," Max says, "there's Mum. She can wait with me while you go in."

"How's the foot, Allie?" Mum asks, plopping herself down on the towel next to me. She picks up my ankle gently and examines my foot. "It looks much better."

"Allie's about to go surfing," Max tells her.

"Um, no, I'm not. Well, I said I would if Max tells me his secret and hugely embarrassing biggest fear."

Mum looks at us and laughs. "Is it what I think it is, Max?"

Max looks embarrassed. "Yes."

"Mum, do you know what it is? Tell me," I say.

"It's not for me to tell. It's up to Max."

"Max, if you tell me, I'll forgive you for taking my diary, as long as you give it back when we get home. I don't forgive you for showing it to Chloe Belton, though— that really sucked."

"Chloe Belton?" Max says, looking puzzled. "What's she got to do with anything? And I told you a million times—I didn't take your dumb diary."

I study Max's face, and I don't know why, but I believe him. Maybe it's because of what happened yesterday. Maybe it's because I realized that it didn't really matter if he had taken my diary or about any of the mean things he's said to me over the years, including telling Chloe Belton about the Pull-Ups, as long as he didn't die. It must have been Willow who took the diary.

"Fine," I say. "I'll try one wave, and then you have to tell me what you're scared of as soon as I get out."

I stomp off to get my board and wet suit and head toward Brad and the Whitewater Warriors. I can't believe I am voluntarily going back in the water.

"Cows," Max yells, stopping me in my tracks.

I spin around to face him.

"Cows? You're scared of cows?"

"Yes," he says, looking around in case Maya is in earshot. "They kill four people every year in England. I read it somewhere."

"They do?"

I think nervously about Mr. Burnham's cows, which suddenly seem less like harmless, grass-chewers and more like deadly killers.

"Yup. Anyway, off you go. Surf's up!" Max says.

"Mooooooo!" I shout at my brother over my shoulder and set off down the beach. I'm so busy checking the sand for jellyfish that I almost walk right into Brad.

"Hey, Allie. Are you coming in? Good for you."

"I promised Max I'd go in for ten minutes and try to 'catch a wave.'" I put "catch a wave" in air quotes so that Brad doesn't think I have started to speak surfer.

"Awesome," he says. "Let's do this!"

"Awesome," I mutter.

I drag the awful wet suit on for what will definitely be the last time. I am never wearing a wet suit again. Brad goes through the dreaded pop-up technique with me on the beach.

"Are you ready to hit the waves?" he asks.

"As I'll ever be."

I walk tentatively out into the water, remembering to check for jellyfish—dead or alive—and start to paddle out. When Brad reaches the swell, he stops to wait for me to catch up. I turn my board around and look back toward the beach. Mum and Max are standing at the edge of the water. Max gives me a thumbs-up. If he could hear me, I'd moo at him again. I know I promised not to tell anyone, but I didn't promise not to laugh at him about it every day.

"The next wave is all yours, girl," Brad shouts. "Paddle!"

I look over my shoulder and paddle frantically, my arms cutting through the water faster than they ever have. Suddenly, the board magically lifts beneath me as the wave catches me—it is definitely not me catching the wave. I push up on my hands, slide one foot next to my knee and the other between my hands, and somehow, miracle of miracles, I manage to stand up. It feels amazing.

"I'm doing it!" I yell a second before I go crashing headfirst into the water.

"That was awesome!" Brad says when I come up coughing and spluttering. "You did it!"

"I fell off," I say, spitting out seawater.

"You bent too far forward. You need to straighten up more. Ready to try again?"

I look at Max and Mum, who are waving and clapping at the water's edge. I only promised Max I'd try one wave. He gives me another thumbs-up.

"Fine," I say. "Let's go."

"I'm so proud of you," Mum says when I get out of the water an hour later. "You were amazing! Wasn't she, Max?"

"Not bad," he says. "It would have been better if you'd managed to stay standing for more than five seconds, but not bad."

"Moo!" I say.

"Hey! You said you wouldn't tell anyone."

"Mum already knows, so she doesn't count."

"Fine, but no one else. Promise?"

"Pinkie swear," I say and link pinkie fingers with my brother.

Mum grins. "I'm going to get Willow and your dad, and then we'd better get back to Canyon View to pack. We've got a flight to catch."

It's time to go home.

CHAPTER THIRTY-THREE

SAGE
IS GOING HOME

"Aquamarine is a stone that can help bring closure to unresolved situations. Do you have unfinished business to settle? If so, aquamarine is the crystal for you." (from *Crystals A–Z*)

It's going to be weird not to have the chickens to feed. This morning Nestle, Nugget, and even Chickpea are all outside, busily scratching the ground and clucking. It's the first time I've seen Chickpea with both her eyes open. The hens cluck happily as they peck at the grain I scatter in front of them. Allie just throws handfuls of it up in the air, but I try to spread it out evenly. Allie told me that chickens like to eat other things besides grain, like pasta, spinach, grapes, and even cheese, but that I should never feed them avocado or chocolate.

"I bet you'd like mac and cheese," I tell the chickens. "Except the one at school because it's gross."

"Talking to yourself? You're getting as bad as Allie."

Ugh, Chloe Belton.

"I'm talking to the chickens, actually," I say, deciding

I don't care what Chloe Belton thinks of me. When your whole world has imploded, the opinion of some stuck-up English girl doesn't seem to matter. "Allie said they like it."

"I wouldn't listen to Allie," she says. "She's such a weirdo."

"I don't think she's weird," I say, turning back to the chickens.

"That's because you hardly know her," Chloe says. "If you did, you'd realize she's a total dork—all that spying stuff she's into, oh, and she seeeeeeriously thinks that Toby South would ever go on a date with her. She wrote all this dumb stuff about how cute he looked in his costume in that stupid school play."

I look up from inspecting Chickpea. "What do you mean, she wrote it?"

"In her diary. It was hidden in there with those disgusting chickens. I'd seen her scribbling in a book and then leaving it in there. It was pretty obvious that it was her diary. I can't wait until school starts so I can tell Toby and the others."

I look at Chloe in disgust. "You went into the henhouse and stole Allie's diary?"

"So what. She shouldn't leave it lying around."

"It wasn't lying around," I say. "It was where she kept it on her own private property. I'd say crawling into a chicken coop in someone else's garden to see if you can find their diary makes you the weirdo, not Allie."

Chloe scowls at me. "Nobody cares what you think."

"Well, you really seem to care a lot about what Allie thinks. Enough to go into the Chick-Inn to steal her diary!"

"I've got way better things to think about than Allie Greenwood."

I smile at her. "Like your fake Italian boyfriend, you mean?"

"Luca is not fake. You're just jealous because you don't have a boyfriend."

"I don't want a boyfriend." I look right at her. "And your Italian boyfriend is one hundred percent fake. My mom saw your mom at Mrs. Armstrong's store the other day and asked her about it, and your mom didn't know what she was talking about and said that you'd been in bed most of your vacation with diarrhea."

It's true that Mom told me she had run into Mrs. Belton in the store, and that Mrs. Belton had said what a shame it was that Chloe missed most of the vacation because she had a terrible stomach flu. My mom, of course, had no idea about Chloe's made-up Italian boyfriend.

Chloe's pretty face flushes an ugly purple. "That's a lie."

I shrug. "Ask your mom if you don't believe me. Oh, and you might want to go and get Allie's diary right now, or I'll tell Allie and Max that you made up your Italian boyfriend—better still, I'll text them the recording I just made of our conversation."

I wave my cell phone at her. "I'm waiting," I say, smiling sweetly. "But you'd better hurry. I've got a plane to catch."

Chloe stomps off inside, her fists clenched tightly at her sides.

I set my phone to record, so I can show her me deleting a file when she hands over the diary. She won't figure out I never recorded our conversation. She's not that smart.

"Here," she says, shoving a battered-looking purple notebook at me. "Take the stupid thing. Now give me your phone."

"No way. I'm not giving you my phone. You can watch me delete the recording, though." I hold up my cell phone to show her and press delete on the file. "There. Gone."

"Ha! Not very smart. Now there's nothing to stop me from telling everyone what's in Allie's diary," Chloe says. "Idiot."

I wave the phone at her. "And there's nothing to stop me sending this recording to Allie and Max and Toby South and whoever else Allie thinks might find it funny.

You don't think I really deleted it, doooooooo you?"

Chloe Belton turns and stomps off into her house.

I smile. Allie would be proud of me.

It's time to go home.

PART FOUR

HOME
AGAIN

ONE YEAR LATER

CHAPTER THIRTY-FOUR

ALLIE
IS IN HER OWN BEDROOM

"1DEAO 1RDIARYO." (from my new diary)

We moved out of Cringle Cottage into a bigger, modern house on the outskirts of the village when Marina was born. Mum and Dad wanted to call the baby Callie (short for California) because that's where Mum got pregnant. BARF! I pointed out that **ONE**, that was a terrible idea because **TWO**, they'd probably think it was funny to tell people why they chose the name, and **THREE**, the poor child would end up hating them because **FOUR**, nobody wants to know where they were conceived, and anyway, **FIVE**, you can't have kids with rhyming names, and I am not being called Allegra.

Marina is quite sweet, considering the last thing I thought I wanted was someone else in the house. She has wispy hair the color of a strawberry, bright brown eyes, and a smattering of freckles. I tried to take her fingerprints when she was about a month old, but they didn't show up well. I bet she has an arch print, just like me. Willow is obsessed with the baby, which is bad for Marina but good for me, as Willow doesn't stalk me all the time now.

Another great thing about the new house is that I don't have to see Chloe Belton every time I go out to feed the chickens. She left our school last term to go to some fancy private school, so I hardly have to see her at all. I love that Sage pretended to record her! Genius. I can't believe Chloe had my diary the whole time. I'm glad I told Max I believed him that day on the beach when he promised me that he hadn't taken it. I'm glad it was Chloe Belton who stole my diary and not my brother or sister.

Max and I still argue, but everything shifted a bit in our family after we got home and then even more when Marina arrived. Our family meetings are mostly okay, except when Bear runs off with the talking stick. Sage says things are better in my family because we're a hexagon now, not a pentagon. It's funny that Sage is the one who solved the mystery of the missing diary and turned out to be the one with code-cracking in her blood. I asked Granny what my great-great-grandmother did during the war. She said she was something called a Land Girl and mostly dug up potatoes. That doesn't sound right at all. I bet she was a spy and potato digging was her cover. That reminds me, I should text Sage to see how long it will be before she arrives. Maybe I'll text her in code—she's getting pretty good at the Bump and Shift code now.

I can't wait to see her.

CHAPTER THIRTY-FIVE

SAGE
IS IN A CAB

"Sunstone is a crystal of self-confidence, hope, light, and joy. Do you want to let your true self shine through? If yes, sunstone is the crystal for you."
(from *Crystals A–Z*)

My homes are a quarter of a mile apart—both in the same direction from school, which is good because it means I don't keep getting on the wrong bus like Nora and Nico still do. Mom and I moved out of Canyon View six months ago, into a house near Dad's. Pandora doesn't hate her basket as much anymore, although she does yowl on her way between Mom's and Dad's places.

My two bedrooms are decorated completely differently. I decided I didn't want my rooms to be identical in both houses like Nora's. I wanted to go to sleep and wake up knowing exactly where I was. My bedroom at Dad's house is similar to the one at Canyon View—mostly white, with a bit of pink. My bedroom at Mom's house is a rainbow of colors. I don't even have my books in alphabetical order—I grouped them by color instead—and I have wind chimes hanging at the window, a bunch of cactus plants on a shelf, and a big, braided rug that feels totally different from the sheepskin rug in my room at Dad's house. If I wake up in the middle of the night to go to the bathroom, I know exactly where I am, even in the dark. That's important.

I put Great-great-great-aunt Lily's Bletchley Park medal in a frame on the wall in the living room at Mom's house next to my great-great-grandparents' wedding picture. I can tell that Allie is jealous that she doesn't have a relative who was an important codebreaker at Bletchley Park. I asked her what her great-great-grandmother did during the war, and she said she can't tell me because it is classified information. I bet she was a spy in Germany, or something really brave like that.

I got an A for my summer project and included a whole section on Bletchley Park. Allie went to visit the museum and took loads of photos for me. She even got some photos of her standing next to an actual Enigma machine. I can't wait to see it in real life. Mom and Dad came to see me present my project at school. They were telling the truth when they said they don't hate each other. To see them together, you'd never think they were divorced. They get on better than they have in ages. Nora overheard her mom tell their next-door neighbor that she thinks my parents might get back together, but

I don't think so. I didn't even have the feeling of the baby bird's wings fluttering when Nora told me. I think my parents are happier now. My mom never even met the lawyer Stephanie Salinas in the end. My parents did their whole divorce online, which Nora and Nico's mom told my mom was a terrible idea, but it seemed to work out okay.

Dad and I haven't decided where we're going to go for vacation this year, but Mom and I are headed back to Little Moleswood. Grandma is coming with us this time, and we're going to visit Bletchley Park with Betty and Allie. Imagine if we'd never gone to Little Moleswood in the first place. We'd never have found out that Lily even existed. Maybe Mr. Armstrong would have left the suitcase in that dusty old attic, and the medal would have stayed hidden forever. And I'd never have met Allie.

We're even staying at Cringle Cottage again. Allie's parents sold it because they wanted a bigger house because of the baby. A family that lives in London bought it, and they rent it out without you having to do a house swap. It's going to be weird to meet Allie's dad and her brother and sisters. Allie says Marina is really annoying, but I don't believe her because she sends me a ton of photos of her.

I should text Allie to tell her we're in the taxi. I hope

she doesn't reply in that annoying Bump and Shift code. I'd better get the copy of *Think Like a Spy* she gave me out of my backpack, just in case.

I can't wait to see her.

ABOUT BLETCHLEY PARK

Bletchley Park is a large house in Buckinghamshire, England, where a top secret team of codebreakers was located during World War II. Over ten thousand people worked there in total secrecy. Many of these extraordinary cryptologists were young women. People who studied languages, chess champions, mathematicians, and people who excelled at solving word puzzles often made good codebreakers. The British government even recruited the winners of a timed cryptic crossword competition, which ran in a British newspaper.

One of the most significant breakthroughs of World War II was when the people working at Bletchley Park cracked the code of the Enigma machine—a machine that Nazi Germany used to encipher top secret messages. The Enigma machine was capable of generating 158 quintillion possibilities. With the code cracked, the Allies were able to decipher the Nazis' top secret messages. The information gained at Bletchley Park was vital to the Allied victory.

Bletchley Park is also the birthplace of modern computing and has helped shape life as we know it today. It is now a museum that you can visit to learn about the wonderful codebreakers who worked tirelessly to crack the Enigma code and who inspired the characters of Betty and Lily in this book. They also served.

Find out more at https://bletchleypark.org.uk.

ACKNOWLEDGMENTS

Someone once told me that if you live in two countries, you never feel quite at home in either place. There is definitely some truth to that. If home is where the heart is, then mine is on both sides of the Atlantic, but even when they are thirty-five hundred miles away, the following people's love makes me feel as if they are right there with me.

My parents, whose unconditional love gave me the best possible start.

My sister, Fay, whose smile feels like home.

My fabulous friends on both sides of the Atlantic whose love, laughter, and wisdom are with me wherever I am. You know who you are!

The middle grade writing community is another place that feels like home—even on Twitter! The readers, writers, teachers, librarians, and booksellers of middle grade stories possess all the hope and heart of the books they love. Thank you for your support and generosity. Thanks to my critique group, who read the draftiest of drafts, give me virtual shoulders to cry on, and are such wonderful cheerleaders. I'm so glad I found you.

To my writing fairy godmother aka my agent, Elizabeth Bewley: I'll be forever grateful for your belief in me and my stories. To my brilliant editor, Tara Weikum: thank you for your guidance, insightful feedback, and nurturing of this book and this author; you and the entire team at HarperCollins are a joy to work with. Special shout-outs to Sarah Homer, Shona McCarthy, Chris Kwon, Jessie Gang, Delaney Heisterkamp, and Anna Bernard for your hard work. A huge thank-you to Oriol Vidal for another stunning cover.

The biggest thank-you goes to the people I spend every day with. To Abel: the best "yes" I ever said. And to Beatrice and Gabriel: I may spend my days writing books but words can never express my love for you two. How lucky I am to have you.

And to my readers: thank you!